ZOMO

THE RABBIT

HUGH STURTON

ZOMO

The Rabbit

DRAWINGS BY PETER WARNER

ATHENEUM   *1966*   NEW YORK

Contents

ZOMO
THE RABBIT

The Animals' Farm

THE ANIMALS once think that it will be a good idea if they all get together and have a farm of their own. The lion and the elephant talk it over between them, and then the lion sends out a summons to all the others, great and small, and orders them to report for work next day.

When the summons reaches Zomo the Rabbit, he isn't at all pleased. He does not like work at the best of times, and if he has to do any, he believes in doing it for himself and not for other people. That night he grumbles about it to his old woman, but a summons from the

3

lion is a summons from the lion and so next morning
he goes along with the others to the place where the
animals always have their meetings.

When they have all assembled, the lion addresses
them. "Now then," he says, "we are going to clear the
bush and make ourselves a farm. You will do a week's
work now, and we shall summon you again later when
it's time for sowing, hoeing and harvest. And we don't
want any scrimshanking."

As the lion says this, he looks so hard at Zomo
that Zomo thinks he is called on to say something, and
so he says, "May the Chief's life be long." And all the
other animals say, "Amen."

Giwa the Elephant now takes charge and leads
the animals off to the place that he and the lion have
chosen for the farm. The leopard is there and the camel
and the giraffe and the bush-cow and the hyena and the
roan-antelope and the warthog and the monkey and the
jackal and the gazelle and the wildcat and the porcupine and the hedgehog and the tortoise and all the other
animals right down to the field-mouse and the dung-
beetle.

"There you are," says the elephant when he has
measured out the work. "I have other things to attend
to now, so I will leave you to get on with the job, but I
will be back this evening to see how you do." With this,
he hurries off as if he is on very urgent business, but as
soon as he is out of sight, he finds the shade of a large
tree and settles down and goes to sleep.

Meanwhile the other animals are out in the sun

trying to clear the bush, but what with arguing among themselves and not being strong enough to pull down the trees, they do not get on at all well. When the elephant comes back in the evening, therefore, he is very cross with them.

"Deadbeats!" he cries. "Do you call this a day's work?" So saying, he starts charging the trees which the others are unable to fell and bowls them over like ninepins. Each time he knocks one down he says "Scrimshankers!" or "Good-for-nothings!" or "Why do I have to do their work as well as my own?" By the time the sun sets, he has flattened the bush over the whole farm.

The animals spend the next six days clearing up the timber that the elephant has felled. When they have finished, the elephant dismisses them. "All right," he says, "you can go home now, but as soon as we get the first rain, I want you all back here for the sowing."

When the first rain falls, the animals all turn out again. The tall ones like the giraffe and the camel go first with long hoes and make holes for the seed. Next come the little ones like the hedgehog and the field-mouse and put the seed into the holes. Then last of all come the heavy ones like the bush-cow and the roan-antelope to cover up the seed in the holes and press the earth down again. All goes well except that Kusu the Field-mouse, who is carrying a bag of seed that is too heavy for him, keeps tumbling into the holes and having to be helped out again. "Ho there up front," he

shouts when he falls in for the third time, "stop dig-
ging pits for us at the back to fall into." But the others
carry on just the same, and by nightfall the sowing is
finished.

After the sowing, the animals all go back to their
homes. By and by the corn appears, and when it is
about two feet high, they turn out again and hoe the
whole farm to get rid of the weeds. Then, when the
rains begin to let up, and the corn starts to ripen, they
meet once again and build three large corn bins to
hold the grain.

At last the corn is ripe, and the elephant sends out
another summons. Next morning the animals assemble
as usual, and the harvest begins. While they are filling
the corn bins, the jackal suddenly thinks of something.
"We all help to grow this corn," he says, "but we do
not yet decide how we will divide it out between us."

"There is only one way," says Kusu the Field-
mouse.

"What's that?" ask the others.

"Why, equal shares of course," says he. At this all the others except the dung-beetle burst out laughing.

"Well, what other way is there?" says the field-mouse, looking very vexed.

"By seniority, of course," says Rakumi the Camel. "Those like the lion and myself who come from old families ought to have bigger shares." But the other animals do not like this idea any more than the field-mouse's, and they begin to shout very loud.

"Ignorant peasants," says the camel and stalks off and sulks.

After this all the animals start talking at once. Kunkuru the Tortoise, who is a hundred and twenty years old, says that the corn ought to be divided out among them according to their ages. Rakumin Dawa the Giraffe, who is seventeen feet tall, says that it ought to be done by height. Zomo the Rabbit, who has sixteen children, apart from the sixty-four who are already grown up, says that what really matters is the number of mouths to be fed.

They are making so much noise with all this argy-bargy that the elephant, who is taking another snooze in the shade, wakes up and comes back to the farm to see what is wrong. When the animals have explained what they are arguing about, they ask him to settle the quarrel.

"Well if I do," says the elephant, "will you accept what I say?"

"We will," say the other animals.

"All right then," says the elephant, "if you want my opinion, there is only one way of dividing the corn."

"What's that?" ask the other animals.

"Well, it's obvious, isn't it?" says the elephant.

"Tell us," say the other animals.

"Why, by weight of course," says the elephant. "What else will it be?"

This causes a bigger hubbub than ever. In the middle of it the lion appears and the quarrel has to be explained all over again. The lion doesn't for the life of him know how to settle it, but Dila the Jackal says that he has an idea.

"All right," says the lion, "let's hear your idea."

"At this time of the year," says Dila, "there is plenty of food for all of us, so let's store our corn for the present and go about our businesses. At the end of the dry season when the hungry time comes round, we will meet here again and decide how the corn is to be divided out."

The animals agree to this, and so the rest of the corn is stored away into the bins and the bins are sealed up. Then, when the lion has appointed a day for them to meet again, they all disperse to their homes.

Soon after this, the lion and the leopard and the giraffe and the bush-cow and the roan-antelope and the warthog and most of the bigger animals go off on their dry-season travels. Giwa the Elephant does not go because it is his turn to stay and keep order among those who remain behind, but he removes himself to the swamp so that he can take the waters, which he says do him good. This only leaves a few people at home such as Kura the Hyena and Zomo the Rabbit and some of the smaller animals such as Bushiya the Hedgehog whose legs are too short to take them away.

Now one day Kura the Hyena goes round to the corn bins to see whether there is anything to be picked up there. The bins are raised up on stones, and he finds that by making a hole in the bottom, he is able to help himself.

Nobody sees Kura doing this, and so when he finishes the first lot he goes back and helps himself to some more. After a while he finishes all the corn in the first bin and broaches the second, and then when

he finishes the second, he broaches the third.

Now each time Kura visits the corn bins he is careful to cover up his tracks. Then he thinks it will be better still if he lays a false trail. So he sweeps up some of Zomo's droppings and scatters them round the bins so that people will think Zomo has been there. "Now my friend," he says, "just explain that away."

By this time it is late in the dry season, and when the appointed day comes round, the animals assemble again at the farm. "Are we all here?" asks the lion, looking round at the others. To make sure, Dila the Jackal, who always acts as usher, begins to call the roll. When it comes to the hyena's name, it is found that he is not in his place.

"Does anyone see Kura?" asks the lion.

"Here I am, Lords of the Bush," says Kura, who now comes panting up with his clothes covered in dust as if he has this very minute returned from his travels.

"Now that we are all here," says the lion, "we must first appoint someone to count the bundles of corn. When we know how many we have we can decide how to divide them up."

It is agreed that Dila the Jackal shall count the bundles, and he goes over to the first bin. He breaks the seal over the opening and puts his head inside. "Why—it's empty," he shouts.

This news causes an uproar among the other animals. They rush up to see if Dila speaks the truth, and then they dash over to look at the second bin. They find that there is no corn left there either. The elephant is now in such a hurry to open the third bin that he staves it in and the animals see that it is empty, too.

"We've been robbed," they cry.

"I know who did it," says Kura. "It is Zomo. Look —here are his droppings all over the place."

"I never," says Zomo, who for once is not guilty. "You know that I will not do such a thing."

"Zomo's been up to his tricks again," say some of the animals like Biri the Monkey and Damisa the Leopard.

"Zomo," says the lion, "it looks mighty black for you. If you did not do it, you must prove who did."

"God give you long life," says Zomo. "I can if you will do as I say."

"Do what?" says the lion.

Zomo tells him that he must have sticks cut all the same length, and that he must give a stick to each animal and lock them all up for the night. "In the morning," he goes on, "you will find that one of the sticks has grown a foot longer than the others. This will show you who takes the corn."

"Very well," says the lion. "Let sticks be prepared as Zomo has said."

When the sticks have been cut and handed round, the animals are locked up for the night. Kura the Hyena is now feeling anxious because he thinks that he will be found out. So he waits until the others have all gone to sleep and then he takes out his knife and cuts a foot off the end of his stick. "Zomo thinks

he is very smart," he says to himself, "but he'll find that I am not born yesterday."

Next morning, when the animals are paraded, the lion doesn't know what to make of the sticks at all. "None of them has grown any longer," he says, "but Kura's somehow seems to have grown shorter." At this, Dila the Jackal goes up and whispers something in his ear. "Oh, so that's it," he says. "Very clever. I wonder how it is that we do not think of it ourselves. But never mind that now—we must deal with Kura."

By this time the hyena is shaking in his shoes. "Kura," roars the lion, "you give yourself away. I pronounce you guilty, you crapulous coffin-robber, and I will deliver sentence myself." So saying, he springs at him and gives him such a thump on the rump that ever since then Kura's hindquarters have been a foot lower than his shoulders.

"Yaroo," bellows Kura and makes a bolt for it. The other animals go after him and give him the biggest thrashing he ever has in his life.

When the lion gets home in the evening, he does not mention Zomo, but tells his wife how clever he has been to find Kura out. She asks him how he does it, and he starts explaining about the stick which grows shorter instead of longer. But then he gets himself into a muddle and forgets what it is that has given Kura away. And so in the end he breaks off and says that it is too difficult for a woman to understand anyway and why can't his wife see about dinner instead of standing there and asking a lot of fool questions.

Zomo Pays
His Debts

Zomo the rabbit is never a great one for work. He will tell you that he likes using his head, not his hands, but the truth is that unless he has to, he will not use either.

One day his wife comes and asks him for money so that she can go and buy food. Zomo puts his hand into his right pocket and it is empty. Then he tries his left pocket and that is empty, too.

"Oho," says his wife, "so that's how it is, is it? Very well—no money, no supper."

14

"I'll go and borrow some," says Zomo.

"Borrow some?" says his wife. "Who d'you think will lend anything to a lazy good-for-nothing like you?"

"Bushiya may," says Zomo. Bushiya is the hedge-hog and he keeps a stall in the market.

"Fiddlesticks!" says his wife. "You owe him for a month's snuff already. Why can't you work like other men," she goes on, "instead of lounging about the house all day and getting under my feet?"

"This is no way to talk to the breadwinner," says Zomo, and with that he picks up his stick and goes out.

Outside the sun is shining, but Zomo is worried at the thought of going without his supper or, worse still, having to do some work. So when he has gone a little way, he sits down on a stump by the side of the road to have a good think. He is sitting there cogitating when Buzuzu the Dung-beetle happens to come by, rolling one of his balls.

" 'Morning, Buzuzu," says Zomo.

" 'Morning, Zomo," says Buzuzu, stopping to mop his brow.

"Busy I see," says Zomo.

"Ah, that I am," says Buzuzu. "Seems to be no end to it."

They talk for a while, and by and by an idea strikes Zomo. "You're a warm man, Buzuzu," he says. "I wonder, can you lend me a thousand till the end of the month? I will not be troubling you normally," he goes on quickly, before Buzuzu can say no, "but I have been lending out my own money lately and it has left me a bit short."

"Well, you know I can't really afford it," says Buzuzu.

"Oh, go on," says Zomo, "I will do the same for you any day if I have any money to lend."

"All right then," says Buzuzu. "When will you pay me back?"

"Friday," says Zomo, "without fail. You come to my house at half past ten, and you shall have your money and a cola-nut into the bargain."

"Very well," says Buzuzu, "but none of your tricks, mind."

"I will not play a trick on you," says Zomo. "You know that."

The beetle now takes Zomo back to his house and counts out a thousand cowries.

"Thank you, Buzuzu," says Zomo when the money has been handed over. "Half past ten, then, next Friday. Don't be late."

"I'll be there," says Buzuzu.

As Zomo is walking home from the beetle's place, his path happens to take him past the house of Zakara the Cock. "Good morning, Zomo," says the cock over the fence. "Where are you off to?"

" 'Morning Zakara," says Zomo. Then another idea strikes him and he adds, "I am just about to drop in for a chat."

"Glad to see you," says Zakara. "Come on in."

So Zomo goes in and has a chat, and before the cock knows what has happened, he finds that he has lent Zomo a thousand, just like Buzuzu.

"Thank you Zakara," says Zomo when the money has been counted out. "Next Friday, then, at the time I say, and you shall have your money and a cola-nut into the bargain."

"I'll be there," says Zakara.

When Zomo leaves the cock's house, he is walking quite jauntily again. What is more, instead of heading for home, he now makes his way to the wildcat's house. " 'Morning Muzuru," he calls out at the gate. "Are you at home?"

"Come on in," says Muzuru. "Glad to see you."

So Zomo goes in, and after a chat with the wildcat about this and that, he borrows a thousand off him, too."

"Thank you Muzuru," says Zomo when the money has been counted out. "Friday, then, at the time I say."

"I'll be there," says Muzuru.

Later in the day Zomo calls on the dog, the hyena, and the leopard, and from each of them he borrows a thousand.

Last of all he goes to the lion's house. "God give you long life," he calls out at the gate.

"Who's that?" asks the lion from within. "Oh, it's you, Zomo, is it? What do you want?"

"Lords of the Bush," says Zomo, "I have come to pay my respects," Being royalty, the lion has to be addressed in the plural.

"Thank you, Zomo, thank you," says the lion.

"And to crave a favor," says Zomo.

"We don't suppose we shall grant it," says the lion, "but don't let us stop you—crave on."

"I am come," says Zomo, "to ask whether you will be graciously pleased to lend me a thousand."

"Lend you a thousand?" says the lion, "What a preposterous idea! If we do, we don't suppose we shall ever see our money again."

"Indeed you will, Lords of the Bush," says Zomo. "You see I am owed six thousand myself. All I need is something to tide me over till Friday when I am paid."

"And if we lend you a thousand," says the lion,

"how much will you pay us back?"

"Twelve hundred," says Zomo. The lion makes no reply but looks away as if he does not hear Zomo say anything.

"Fifteen hundred then," says Zomo. The lion shakes his head but still does not deign to say anything.

"All right, two thousand," says Zomo.

"Done," says the lion so quickly that Zomo wonders whether he offers too much. But all he says is that he will repay the lion at noon on Friday

"Very well," says the lion, "we shall be passing your house then and we will look in. But we warn you, Zomo," he goes on, "none of your tricks or you will be sorry for it."

"God give you victory," says Zomo. "Who am I to play tricks on anyone, let alone your lordships?"

Zomo now has seven thousand cowries in his pocket, and he goes off looking like the cat who swallows the cream.

"Well," says his wife when he reaches home, "how have you got on?"

"I told you that I'd bring back some money," says Zomo, "and I have. There you are—seven thousand cowries."

"I hope you know how you're going to pay it back," says his wife.

"Leave it to me," says Zomo.

When Friday comes round, Buzuzu the Dung-beetle arrives at Zomo's house on the dot of time.

"Peace be with you," he sings out at the gate.

"Come on in," says Zomo, "I am expecting you."

"Money ready?" asks Buzuzu.

"Of course," says Zomo, "but come and sit down first. Here—let me offer you a cola-nut."

So they sit down together and chew cola-nuts and talk of this and that. As they are chatting, they hear someone else arrive at the gate.

"Who is that?" asks Buzuzu.

"It sounds to me like Zakara the Cock," says Zomo.

"In that case," says Buzuzu, "I think I'll be going."

"But your money," says Zomo. "I haven't paid you yet."

"Never mind about that now," says Buzuzu.

"What's the matter?" asks Zomo.

"Nothing," says Buzuzu, who by this time is hopping about like a man who has an ant up his trouser leg. "It's just that I remember something that my mother told me when I was still small."

"What did your mother tell you?" asks Zomo.

"She told me not to trust that Zakara," says Buzuzu, "and above all she told me to see that I am never left alone with him."

"If you don't wish to meet Zakara," says Zomo, "I'll let you out at the back door."

"That will be fine," says Buzuzu.

"I am forgetting, though," says Zomo. "I can't do this any more."

"Why ever not?" asks Buzuzu.

"Because I had to sell my back yard to Bushiya the Hedgehog," says Zomo, "on account of my owing him money that I was unable to repay. And now," he goes on, "if ever I want to use it, Bushiya makes me pay a toll." Of course the only word of truth in all this is that Zomo owes Bushiya money, which is well known to all.

"Never mind," says Buzuzu. "If it's not too much, I will pay."

"It's rather a lot," says Zomo, "but you know what a skinflint Bushiya is."

"How much?" says Buzuzu, thinking it will be fifty or maybe a hundred.

"Two thousand," says Zomo.

"Two thousand!" says Buzuzu like a man who does not believe his ears. "Why, this is robbery."

All this time Zakara the Cock is dismounting from his horse in front of Zomo's house. He comes to the gate and sings out, "Anyone at home?"

"Coming Zakara," shouts Zomo.

"Quick, let me out of here," says the beetle. "We'll cancel the thousand you owe me, and I'll give you a thousand instead."

"If you insist," says Zomo, pocketing the money.

As soon as the beetle has gone out by the back door, Zomo returns to the front and lets the cock in. "Welcome, Zakara," he says, "I am expecting you."

"Got the money ready?" asks Zakara.

"It is here," says Zomo tapping his pocket, "but come in first and let me offer you a cola-nut."

So they sit down together and chew cola-nuts and talk of this and that. And then, just when Zakara is ready to take his money and go, they hear the noise of someone else arriving at the gate.

"Who is that?" asks Zakara.

"I'm not sure," says Zomo, "but it sounds to me like Muzuru the Cat."

"I'll be off then," says Zakara.

"But your money," says Zomo. "I haven't paid you yet."

"Never mind about that now," says Zakara, who by this time has a feeling in his belly as if the hairy caterpillar that he swallowed earlier that morning has come to life and is going on a tour of inspection.

"What's the matter?" asks Zomo.

"Nothing," says Zakara. "It's just that I remember something that my mother told me when I was still small."

"What did your mother tell you?" asks Zomo.

"She told me not to trust that Muzuru," says Zakara, "and above all she told me never to put temptation in his way. She said, if there's one thing wildcats can't resist, it's temptation."

Well, the long and the short of it is that the cock like the beetle is in such a hurry to be gone that instead of collecting a thousand from Zomo, as he expects, he is glad to pay a thousand to get out of the back door before the cat gets in at the front.

The same thing happens with all the other animals. The cat is glad to pay a thousand so as not to meet the dog; the dog is glad to pay a thousand so as not to meet the hyena; the hyena is glad to pay a thousand so as not to meet the leopard; and the leopard is glad to pay a thousand so as not to meet the lion.

When Zaki the Lion appears at noon, Zomo lets the leopard out of the back door and hurries round to the front. "God give you victory," he says, doing obeisance and acting very respectful.

"Amen," says the lion. "Got the money ready?"

"It's here," says Zomo, handing over the two bags that the leopard and the hyena have just given him.

"Lucky for you, Zomo," says the lion, pocketing

the money. "Lucky for you."

As soon as the lion has gone, Zomo's wife comes out of the kitchen. "Well," she asks, "were you able to pay them off all right?"

"I just managed it," said Zomo, "but it cleans me right out, so don't come asking me for any house-keeping money."

With this, he picks up his stick and saunters away, hoping that his old woman will not notice how his pockets are bulging. What's more, as soon as he is out of sight, he doubles round to the hedgehog's stall in the market. There he pays off all he owes and lays in enough snuff and cola-nuts to keep him happy for a month.

That same evening, when his wife has put the children to bed, she comes in and finds him chewing cola-nuts and filling his snuff-box.

"Where do you get the snuff and cola-nuts?" she asks.

"Oh, didn't I tell you?" says Zomo. "Zaki the Lion gave them to me when I paid him back this morning. Yes sir. And d'you know what he says to me? 'Zomo,' he says, 'you're the only man in these parts who ever pays his debts. You're an example, you are, to all these other lowborn layabouts who call themselves my subjects.' "

So saying, Zomo spits out the remains of his cola-nut and takes such a large pinch of snuff that he sneezes three times.

The Well

EACH YEAR when the dry season comes round, a lot of the animals go away for four or five months. Some go to see relations living in different parts of the country, and others like Gizo the Spider, who can ply a trade, go to places where they know they will get good profits. The rest, who have no trades to ply and are not on speaking terms with their relations, go off to trade as best they can.

Now each year when the season for these expeditions draws near, Zomo tells his wife that this time he is really going to go, too. One year he says he means to

26

go to Keffi, where he hears the coco-yams are very sweet. Another year he tells her that he means to study to be a whitesmith because he hears that the work is not hard and that down Bida way the whitesmiths earn big money making armlets and anklets for the girls. Somehow, though, when the time comes, there is always a reason why he cannot tear himself away from home. "Never mind," he then says to his wife, "I will go next year instead."

One year, when the rains are beginning to ease up, Zomo tells his wife that as soon as the harvest is finished, he will be off on his travels. He says he is going to Gwanja.

"What are you going to go there for?" asks his wife, who has her doubts as to whether he will ever go anywhere.

"What for?" says Zomo. "Why to trade of course —you don't think I will walk five hundred miles for exercise, do you?"

His wife has heard all this before. "What are you going to trade this time?" she asks.

"Well, I have an idea," says Zomo. "I think I will take a donkeyload of embroidered saddlecloths down to Gwanja, and when I have sold them, I will buy two baskets of cola-nuts to bring back. I will double my money each way, and so if I borrow five thousand from Bushiya to start off with, I will have—let's see, twice five is ten and twice ten is twenty—I'll have twenty thousand when I get back."

"Well, we can do with that," says his wife.

For a week or two Zomo is very keen on his new idea. He arranges to borrow five thousand cowries from Bushiya the Hedgehog and makes a lot of other preparations for his journey. Then one day he comes home and tells his wife that it is all off.

"Well," she says, "what goes wrong this time?"

"I have been talking to Maiki the Griffon," he says, "and you know he goes to all these places."

"Well, what does he tell you?" asks his wife.

"He says it's no good taking saddlecloths to Gwanja," says Zomo, "because they don't have any horses there."

"Well, can't you take something else," asks his wife, "and still buy cola-nuts to bring back?"

"I can," says Zomo, "except that Maiki says that they haven't got any cola-nuts there either."

In the end Zomo promises his wife that he will plan another expedition for the following year. In the meantime, he says that all the preparations he has been making have worn him out and, if she expects him to get the harvest in, he will have to have a fortnight's rest.

When he has made this point, Zomo saunters round to see the hedgehog. "Bushiya," he says, "I have to change my plans. It is no good taking saddlecloths to Gwanja because they do not have any horses there."

"Well," says Bushiya, "what are you going to take instead?"

"I think I will take snuff," says Zomo, who is running short of snuff at home; but he does not tell Bushiya that he has given up the idea of going to Gwanja.

"It's a mighty long way to take snuff," says Bushiya.

"Well, maybe I'll take some cola-nuts as well," says Zomo, who is also running short of cola-nuts.

"But you are going to bring cola-nuts back," says Bushiya.

"Oh, so I am," says Zomo. "I am forgetting. Well then, we'll have to stick to snuff, won't we?"

So the hedgehog measures out snuff to the value of five thousand cowries, enough to fill a couple of large calabashes, and Zomo waits till his wife is out of the house so that he can cart it home and hide it under the bed without her seeing.

Usually the lion and the elephant take it in turns to go away for the dry season. If the lion goes one year, the elephant stays at home to keep the other animals in order. The next year the elephant will go, and the lion will stay behind.

But this year it so happens that they both have to be away together. The next in seniority is Damisa the Leopard, and he now says that, although it is very inconvenient for him, duty is duty and so he will stay and keep order. When the other animals hear this, they are not at all pleased because Damisa has a mean nature and is much given to bossing people about.

Sure enough, as soon as he knows that the lion and the elephant are out of the way, Damisa summons all the animals to his house, "I'm in charge here now," he says, "and expect you to see that I don't want for anything. You can take it in turns to do this," he goes on, "and if I'm not satisfied with any of you, I shall know what to do."

"But," says Gwanki the Roan-antelope, "the lion and the elephant never make us do this."

When he hears what the roan-antelope has to say, Damisa gives a very ugly scowl and says that for this Gwanki can be first on duty and bring him all his meals for the next week. Then he makes the others draw lots to see when their turn will come.

When the leopard has dismissed them and the animals are on their way home, Bushiya the Hedgehog comes up and speaks to Zomo. "Hullo," he says. "I did not expect to see you here today. I have been thinking that you are in Gwanja."

"I wish I were," says Zomo.

"Which week did you draw?" asks Bushiya.

"Fourth," says Zomo. "How about you?"

"Fifth," say Bushiya. "By the way," he goes on, "since you did not go to Gwanja, when will you pay me back that five thousand?"

"Next week," says Zomo.

"Well don't forget," says Bushiya. "I shall need it before it is my turn to feed Damisa."

"All right, all right," says Zomo. "I'll remember."

Zomo is not the worrying kind, and during the next week or two, if it were not for the hedgehog, he would have forgotten all about his troubles. But as it is, he gets no chance because a week later Bushiya comes back to tell him what a bad time Gwanki the Roan-antelope is having while he is looking after the leopard. "If it is costing him a penny," he says, "it is costing him ten thousand. Which reminds me," he goes on, "what about the five thousand you owe me?"

"Next week," says Zomo.

"But you said that last week," says Bushiya.

When next week comes round, Bushiya is back to tell Zomo what a bad time Damo the Iguana has while he is looking after the leopard. "If it were not for that armor-plating of his," he says, "Damo would be a dead man. Which reminds me," he goes on, "what about the five thousand you owe me?"

"Next week," says Zomo, "without fail."

"But you said that last week," says Bushiya. "And the week before."

When the next week comes round, Bushiya is more agitated than ever when he calls on Zomo. "How many ears have you got?" he asks.

"Two," says Zomo.

"Well, find yourself two more and listen to this," says Bushiya. "Damisa is cross because the giraffe only brings him vegetables and fruit instead of meat, and he gives him such a beating that now the giraffe has to go to a bone-setter to have his neck straightened out."

Zomo sees that Bushiya is going to ask for the money he owes, and so he gets his word in first. "Look, Bushiya," he says, "if we go on as we are, we shall all be ruined. What we must do is find a way of getting rid of Damisa."

"But how can we do that?" asks Bushiya.

"I will think of something," says Zomo, "if you and the others make it worth my while."

"What's your price?" asks Bushiya.

"Five thousand," says Zomo.

"Well, that sounds reasonable," says Bushiya. "Let's see now, counting me there are ten to come, so that's five hundred apiece. I think we can run to that, Zomo."

"You do not take my meaning," says Zomo. "When I say five thousand, I mean five thousand each."

"But that is fifty thousand," says Bushiya, falling off his stool in astonishment. "Why, Zomo, you are worse than Damisa."

"A man must live," says Zomo. "Take it or leave it."

Bushiya says that fifty thousand is a whale of a lot of money, and he will have to have a meeting with the others. But he is back next morning with a promise that if Zomo can get rid of Damisa the Leopard, he and his friends will pay him forty-five thousand, being fifty thousand less the five thousand which Zomo already owes.

"It's a deal," says Zomo. "Now go away and let me think."

Zomo's turn to feed the leopard starts on Friday. On Thursday he goes to the pantry and collects some bowls and calabashes and smears food over them, as if they have been used at a meal. He makes these up into a head-load and puts them ready for the morning.

Next day he gets up before it is light and sets off carrying his load on his head. When he reaches the crossroads where the well is, he does not turn off towards the leopard's house, but stops by a large tree that grows on the edge of the clearing. There he unties his load and scatters the bowls and the calabashes about higgledy-piggledy at the foot of the tree. Then he climbs up into the branches and sits down to wait.

By and by, the sun comes up and the other animals begin to appear and go about their business. At first there is no sign of the leopard, but after an hour or two, sounds of yawning and growling and grinding of teeth show that he is becoming impatient for his breakfast. Zomo hears these noises but keeps right on sitting in his tree and saying nothing. This goes on for some time, and then it stops and next minute Damisa himself comes into sight, looking so bad-tempered that the animals who meet him on the path dive into the bush and thank their stars that they are not in Zomo's shoes.

As for Zomo, as soon as he sees Damisa, he starts hollering, "Help!" and "Rescue!" and "Save me!" When he hears the shouts, Damisa goes over to the tree and sees Zomo sitting up there in the branches. "Zomo," he says, looking as black as thunder, "why do I get no breakfast this morning?"

"God give you victory," cries Zomo, "it is not my fault that I am late. Look at these dishes by your feet."

Damisa now looks down and sniffs at the bowls and calabashes.

"Do you see that meat dish?" Zomo asks. "Well, I had a fine haunch of venison on that. And the big calabash—that was full of milk gruel. And the two bowls—they had butter and honey in them. There were snuff and cola-nuts too."

"Well, where is it all?" says Damisa.

"God give you long life," says Zomo, "I've been robbed of it."

"Robbed of it?" roars Damisa. "Do you mean to say that one of these scavenging swabs has the impudence to steal my breakfast? It must be that hyena."

"No," says Zomo, "it isn't Kura."

"Well, that warthog then," says Damisa. "He has no respect for his betters."

"No," says Zomo, "it isn't Gyado."

"Who is it then?" cries Damisa. "Just tell me, and

I'll go and break every bone in his body." He is making so much noise with his roaring, that animals are now running up from all sides, and a crowd is forming.

"God give you victory," says Zomo, "it is another leopard. Just like Your Honor, he is, except he seems even bigger and stronger."

"We'll see about that," roars Damisa, as much as to say that if it is his own father he is still ready to carve him up. "Just you show me which way he goes, and I'll show you who is the boss round here."

"Well," says Zomo, "after he takes my stuff, he goes over to the well and I do not see him come out again. Just think of all that lovely venison!" he adds . with a sigh.

When he hears this, Damisa gives another very ugly growl, bounds over to the well, and glares down. At the bottom what does he see but another leopard glaring back at him. "Who do you think you are?" he asks.

"Who do you think you are?" asks the other leopard. Damisa does not at all like the way he sneers when he says this.

"And what do you mean by eating my breakfast?" shouts Damisa.

"And what do you mean by eating my breakfast?" the other leopard shouts back. Damisa thinks that the tone of voice in which this is said is very disrespectful, and so he scowls down without blinking, but the other leopard scowls right back and does not blink either.

"I can see that I'll have to teach you a lesson,"

roars Damisa. "You impudent, puffed-up, pock-marked Popinjay."

"You impudent, puffed-up, pock-marked Popinjay," roars back the other leopard.

All this answering back is more than Damisa can stand, and so without more ado, he springs at the other leopard.

When Damisa takes off, he forgets that the well is forty foot deep, and he doesn't realize that there is only a foot of water at the bottom. When he hits it, he is traveling so fast that he goes clean through it and his head and shoulders sink right into the mud underneath where they stick fast. When the other animals dash over to find out what becomes of him, all they see is his rump sticking out of the water and his hind legs kicking about. It takes him a couple of minutes to get right way up again, and then he starts hollering, but the mud, which goes up his nose and down his throat, keeps making him choke. "Help!" he roars. *Glug-glug.* Rescue!! *Glug-glug.* Get me out of . . . *Glug-glug.*"

When the animals up top see him smothered in mud and hear him glug-gluging, they roll about holding their sides. Damisa keeps right on hollering, though, and promising them the earth if only they will get him out. Very meek and mild he is, too, for a change, but Zomo isn't going to help him and none of the other animals will take the risk either. So in the end his old woman has to come and fish him out, and that doesn't help matters much because she gives him the rough side of her tongue for making himself a laughing-stock and asks how can she face the neighbors now? So the very same night they pack their bags and go away, and no one sees them again until the next rains.

As for Zomo, he is very popular with the other animals until they find out that he does not mean to let them off the money they promise to pay. Then some of them, like Rakumi the Camel and Bunsuru the Billy-goat, go about saying that he is too clever by half and very mean into the bargain.

But this does not worry Zomo because he now has an answer for his old woman when she nags him about going to Gwanja to earn some money. "Why go all that way for twenty thousand," he says, "when you can stay at home and make fifty thousand?"

Kumurchi's Poultry Farm

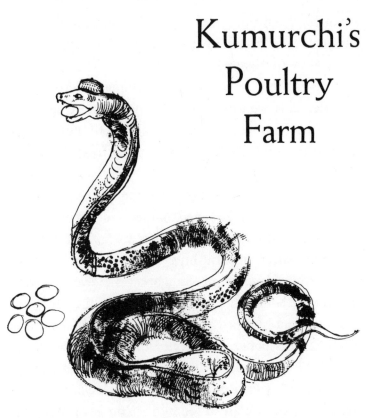

No ONE ever thinks that Kumurchi the Black Cobra has a nice nature, and the most you can say for him is that he keeps himself to himself. But one year a change comes over him, and instead of minding his own business he starts minding other people's.

The trouble all begins when he discovers that he likes eating eggs. After this he starts sending his wife down to the market two or three times a week to buy a dozen at a time. This suits him all right, but his old woman doesn't like it one bit because it runs away with her housekeeping money. So one day she speaks to him about it. "I am thinking," she says, "that we can save ourselves a lot of money if we keep our own hens."

"How so?" says Kumurchi.

"Well, they won't cost us anything to feed," says his wife, "and we won't have to buy any more eggs."

"But hens cost a lot of money to buy," says Kumurchi, "and where is that coming from, I should like to know."

"There are more ways of getting what you want," says his wife, "than going to market and buying it."

"Aha," says Kumurchi, " I see what you mean."

Soon after this Bushiya the Hedgehog happens to be coming back from the market one evening with a couple of hens, which he gets from Biri the Monkey. It is dusk, and he just reaches the stretch of the path where it runs between banks of thorn when suddenly Kumurchi slides out of the bushes and bars his way.

"Oh, it's you, Kumurchi," says Bushiya, trying to sound as if he is glad to see him. "You gave me quite a fright."

"Nice hens you have there," says Kumurchi.

"Yes," says Bushiya. "Biri came in for tobacco today, and since he had no cash, I took these in exchange."

"Biri?" cries Kumurchi, pretending to be surprised.

"Why, what's the matter?" asks Bushiya.

"What's the matter?" says Kumurchi, spreading his hood and acting as if he grows angry. "I'll tell you what's the matter. That monkey owes me two hens for a month or more. Only last week I saw him about them, and he promised to let me have them today. Now he goes and gives them to you."

"I'm sorry," says Bushiya. "I did not know this or I would not have taken them."

"It's no good being sorry," says Kumurchi. "The question is what are you going to do about it?" With this he scowls at Bushiya as if he catches him stealing the eggs that his old woman lays at home, which Kumurchi is known to prize mighty high on account of their being full of little cobras. As for Bushiya, he knows that when Kumurchi looks like this it is no good arguing, and so he just hands the hens over and goes his way.

A few days later Biri the Monkey comes to market again, and Bushiya tells him what has happened and asks for his money in place of the hens that he gave up to Kumurchi. But Biri says that he never owed Kumurchi a penny, let alone two hens, and that anyway Kumurchi is the last man he will bilk except perhaps Kada the Crocodile.

"I don't understand it," says Bushiya. "Perhaps Kumurchi made a mistake."

"Mistake my foot," says Biri. "He swindled you, and that is all there is to it."

Bushiya is still trying to pluck up courage to go and ask Kumurchi for his hens when Kumurchi plays the same trick on Gafiya the Bandicoot. After that it is the turn of the gazelle, the ground-squirrel, and the porcupine. Until now Kumurchi never owned a hen

in his life, as is well known to all, but by the time the
rains come round he has fifteen to twenty running
about his paddock. In fact, except for Zomo, who likes
soft-boiled eggs next after cola-nuts and snuff, there is
not a denizen in those parts with so much poultry
round the house as Kumurchi. "And none of them
honestly come by," says Bushiya, who is still feeling
sore.

The next thing that happens is that all the animals swindled by Kumurchi hold a meeting to talk
about laying a complaint.

"We mustn't take this lying down," says Bushiya,
"or he will diddle us again. I vote we all go along
together and tell Kumurchi exactly what we think of
him."

"Good idea," say the others.

But when it comes to settling who is to do the
talking, each thinks that one of the others ought to
do it. As they cannot agree about this, they decide to
go and see the lion instead.

The lion hears what they have to say and then
asks them if they have any witnesses.

"No," says Bushiya, "we have no witnesses because we are alone when it happens."

The lion looks rather relieved to hear this. "Then
I'm sorry," he says, "but I can't help you."

"But," says Bushiya, "our hens are there in Kumurchi's paddock—we can recognize them."

"One hen looks very like another," says the lion,
"and if you have no witnesses, it will only be your

word against his."

With this he dismisses them, and they leave the audience chamber. "I bet you," says Bushiya afterwards, "that he would settle the case quickly enough if it were anyone but Kumurchi. Until now I never saw him miss the chance of making his commission."

Zomo is never one to look for trouble and takes care not to get mixed up in this quarrel. He steers clear of Kumurchi the Cobra, especially around dusk, and tells his wife to see that their hens do not stray. But one day two of them get loose, and the next time he sees them, there they are in the cobra's paddock with the others.

When Zomo goes round to get his hens back, Kumurchi doesn't seem at all pleased. In fact he looks at Zomo as if he is a fly who falls into the milk. He says that he knows every one of his hens by sight (though actually they all look the same to him, and he can never tell one from another) and that there is not one in the paddock which does not belong to him or his wife. In any case, he goes on, Zomo's hens have no business to be on his land, and if he ever finds any of them there in the future it will be the worse for them. "And for you, too," he adds, looking at Zomo in a way that is not at all warm or neighborly. After this Zomo and Kumurchi are hardly on speaking terms.

Now as it happens Kumurchi has a field that lies between his house and Zomo's. This year he plants it with bulrush-millet, and of course, if there is one thing that hens like more than any other it is bulrush-millet. By and by the harvest comes round. As soon as he sees that Kumurchi has cut his millet, Zomo shuts up all his hens so that they will not get at it. You know how it is with hens, though—before long one of them gets loose and makes a beeline for the millet.

Now Kumurchi has been half hoping that this will happen and has told his wife to keep a sharp lookout. As soon as she sees Zomo's hen in the field, she calls out to the old man, and he dashes across and gives it a bite and that is the end of the hen. When Zomo arrives a little later, the bird has already turned up its toes and Kumurchi is sitting there looking as if he has just come into some money.

This is the third hen that Zomo has lost, and he comes to the conclusion that it is time for him to sit down and have a good think. So he settles himself under the *chediya* tree as usual and thinks and thinks again for the whole of the afternoon. Then just as the sun is setting he suddenly jumps up and says to himself,

"Of course—why didn't I think of it before?" At supper that night he is as merry as a grig, and his wife thinks he must have won a bet. But all he will say is that he wants a long piece of string and an early call.

Next morning Zomo gets up before it is light and makes his way down to the cobra's hen-house. When he gets there, he ties one end of the string to the bar that keeps the door shut, covers up his tracks, takes the other end and hides himself in the bushes.

Soon afterwards it begins to grow light. At this the cobra's rooster starts crowing, and the hens flutter about as if they wish to be up and doing. Zomo waits until the sun comes up, and then he pulls the string. As soon as the bar falls away, the door of the hen-house flies open; and as soon as the door flies open, the rooster and the hens come streaming out. They know about the millet, of course, and so they make a beeline for the farm just as Zomo's hen did. In fact by the time the cobra family starts stirring, the hens are pecking and scratching as hard as they can go.

Old Kumurchi was up late the night before and he is sleepy and in no hurry to get up. So his wife is the first to put her head out, and as soon as she spots the hens, she sings out and tells the old man that Zomo's chickens are on their land again. This is the best news Kumurchi has for a long time. He comes out of his house like an arrow out of a bow, and before you can say knife, he is picking off the hens faster than they are picking off the millet. In fact by the time Zomo has sneaked back to his own house, it is all over and the farm is looking like a battlefield.

Soon after this, a message reaches Zomo up at his house. It says that Kumurchi the Cobra sends his greetings to Zomo the Rabbit and will be obliged if he will remove his poultry from the millet farm.

To this Zomo replies by saying that he returns greetings to Kumurchi the Cobra and that he has received his message but cannot understand it.

Back comes a second message from Kumurchi saying that if Zomo will survey the millet farm, the meaning of the message will be clear.

To this Zomo replies saying that he has already surveyed the millet farm but he still cannot understand the message.

Back comes a third message from Kumurchi saying that if Zomo will examine his own hen-house as well as the millet farm, the meaning of the message will become clear and that Kumurchi will take it as a favor if he will then remove his poultry as requested the first time.

To this Zomo returns a message saying that he has already examined his hen-house and that his hens, thank God, are safe and well.

When he gets this last message, Kumurchi cannot make it out at all. Then a horrid doubt strikes him, and he turns to his wife. "I suppose you're sure," he says, "that these hens in the farm really are Zomo's."

"Who else's will they be?" says his wife.

"But Zomo says his hens are all right," says Kumurchi.

"They must be his," says his wife. "No one else has so many."

"You're forgetting ours," says Kumurchi. "Have you looked at them today?"

When his wife says that she has not, they both fly out to the hen-house as fast as they can cover the ground. They find the door open, of course, and the hen-house empty.

Well, as Zomo remembered to untie the string and take it away with him, Kumurchi never finds out how the door of the hen-house got open. For a long time he thinks that Zomo had something to do with it, but in the end decides that it has all been the fault of his old woman. "You ropy old creep," he cries. "First you talk me into putting my capital into poultry, and then you make me lose it all."

For months afterwards it makes him so mad, just thinking about it, that he feels like biting her, too, only he knows that it will do no good on account of her being just as poisonous as he is, if not more so.

Bunsuru's Grave

THEY SAY there is nothing like a debt for coming between friends, and this is how it is with Zomo and
Bunsuru the Billy-goat.

The trouble starts because Bunsuru is one of
those who promised to subscribe five thousand if
Zomo can stop Damisa the Leopard from oppressing
the other denizens. At the time he is ready to promise
anything, but as soon as the danger passes, it is a very
different story, and he starts thinking of excuses for
not paying.

Bunsuru is still thinking when one day Rakumi

the Camel drops in on him. Usually Rakumi is too high and mighty to have any truck with such people as goats, but now he looks in because he too has promised to subscribe five thousand for Zomo and he hopes to find a way of getting out of it.

When they finish greeting one another, they start talking about this and that and after a while Rakumi comes to the point and asks Bunsuru whether he means to pay Zomo. Bunsuru says he doesn't think he will, and Rakumi says that in that case he won't either. This is a great load off their minds because five thousand is a lot of money to be paying out with nothing to show at the end of it. After all, they tell one another, when all is said and done, what is Zomo but a tuppenny-ha'penny rabbit who has no respect for his elders and betters?

Now for most of the dry season Zomo has plenty of money, and so he does not bother his head about the people like Bunsuru and Rakumi who do not pay him what they owe. But by the time the hot weather comes round again, he has run through all his cash and Bushiya the Hedgehog is putting his snuff and cola-nuts on the slate again. This reminds Zomo about the debts, and the next time he is passing the goat's house, he thinks that it will be a good chance to collect. So he stops at the gate and sings out: "Hello Bunsuru, are you in?"

At first there is no answer, though Zomo can hear people talking in low voices inside, but by and by the old nanny comes to the door.

"Good morning, Ma'am," says Zomo. "Is Bunsuru in?"

"There, isn't that bad luck?" says the nanny. "He is gone to get some medicine, and you just miss him."

"Never mind," says Zomo. "I only come to remind him about the five thousand he owes."

The second time he calls, the kids are playing games and making a great noise, but as soon as the nanny hears that it is Zomo outside, she shuts them up. "You ought to be ashamed of yourselves," she says to them in a loud voice. "Making all that noise when your poor father is lying at death's door." Then she comes to the gate and tells Zomo that Bunsuru is home again but too ill to see anyone.

Zomo says he is very sorry to hear it and will come back in three days time to see if he is better.

The third time Zomo calls, he is just walking up to the house when suddenly all the kids start boohooing as if they lose their father or their mother. Sure enough, when the nanny comes to the door, she tells Zomo that Bunsuru is no more. Then she starts boo-hooing, too, and there is so much noise in the house that Zomo cannot hear himself think. By and by the old nanny stops crying and begins to talk.

"You remember how ill he was last time you called?" she says. "Well, he just sank and sank until yesterday evening he went the way of all flesh."

Zomo says he has not heard the news and it comes as a great shock to him.

"He spoke of you on his deathbed," the nanny

goes on. "He says that when you come round again, I am to be sure to show you his grave." So saying, she leads Zomo out to the back and shows him a new grave, which looks as if it is a good fit for Bunsuru.

Now the fact is that old Bunsuru is not dead at all but only trying to play a trick on Zomo. The day before he made his children dig a grave and early in the morning, before it was light, he climbed down into it. His wife then covered it over with a roof of old calabashes, and the kids piled the earth back on top so that it looks like a real grave.

When the nanny takes Zomo out to see the grave, old Bunsuru is right there inside. He has a bowl of milk gruel by his side, and he is sitting there smoking his pipe, as snug and comfortable as you please.

As the nanny shows Zomo the grave she says, "Bunsuru keeps thinking of you right up to the end on account of the five thousand he owes you."

Down in the grave old Bunsuru can hear every word that they are saying up top. At this he nods his head and strokes his beard.

"Yes, Sir," the nanny goes on. "That debt is really on his conscience. 'Tell Zomo' he says to me, 'that it is too late to pay him in this world but that I will settle up in the next.' Those are the very last words he speaks."

When old Bunsuru hears this down below, he shakes all over with laughing. "Settle up in the next world," he says to himself. "Very good. Very good indeed."

Zomo says that he is mighty sad that Bunsuru has been taken before his time and touched to think that his last thoughts have been of him. "All the same," he goes on, "as an old friend you must let me give you a bit of advice." The nanny says that as she is a poor widow now, she will need all the advice she can get.

"It's about this grave," says Zomo. "You know what a coffin-robber Kura the Hyena is. If he gets to hear that the remains of poor Bunsuru are down here, he will have them out in no time."

Bunsuru never thinks of this, and it makes him

sit up in the grave with such a jerk that he bumps his head on the calabashes, which ring with a hollow sound.

"What is that?" asks Zomo.

"What is what?" asks the nanny, pretending that she does not hear anything.

"I think I hear something moving down below," says Zomo.

"How can that be," says the nanny, "when poor Bunsuru is lying there stiff and cold?"

When he hears this, old Bunsuru nods his head again as much as to say that he can't tell fibs better than that himself.

"Perhaps I am mistaken," says Zomo. "Anyway," he goes on, "tomorrow you must send the children out to cut thorn. If you pile it up on top of the grave, it will keep Kura out."

"But what about tonight?" asks the nanny.

"It's too late to do anything about tonight," says Zomo. "We shall just have to take a chance on that."

The sun is already low when Zomo leaves the goat's place, and he hurries straight round to see Aku the Parrot.

"Aku," he says when he finds him, "I have a proposition to put to you."

"What is it?" asks Aku.

"If you will help me tonight," says Zomo, "we can make a good profit."

"What's in it for me?" asks Aku.

"A quarter of whatever we make," says Zomo.

"Done," says Aku. "What do you want me to do?"

"Meet me by the silk-cotton tree," says Zomo, "as soon as the moon rises."

When the moon rises, Zomo and Aku meet by the silk-cotton tree and set off in the direction of the goat's house.

"Can you make a call like Kura the Hyena?" asks Zomo as they go along.

"Of course I can," says Aku. "Like him or anyone else."

"Good," says Zomo. "And can you growl like him and gnash your teeth?"

"Just shut your eyes and listen to this," says Aku.

"Gggrrr, Snap-crunch, Gggrrr."

"Very good indeed," says Zomo, opening his eyes again. "You give me quite a turn."

"What do you wish me to do?" asks Aku.

"It is quite simple," says Zomo, and whispers something in Aku's ear.

"All right," says Aku. "Tell me when to begin?"

"You can begin right away," says Zomo.

At this Aku draws a deep breath and starts sending out calls that sound like Kura the Hyena when his belly is empty. The calls carry to the goat's place where the nanny is about to open the grave and let old Bunsuru out. As soon as she hears them, she takes fright and bolts back to the house and barricades herself in with the children.

As for old Bunsuru, he thinks that Kura the Hyena is coming after him, and if there is one of his neighbors whom he does not wish to meet on a dark night, it is Kura the Hyena. So he crouches down in a corner of the grave and prays as he never prays before that Kura will go past. But the calls get louder and louder, and then before he knows where he is, he hears someone moving about up top. There is a scratching and a scrabbling and then another sound which makes his blood run cold—*Gggrrr, Snap-crunch, Gggrrr.*

For a while old Bunsuru is so scared that he can't move. Then he suddenly finds his voice and starts bellowing so loud that he nearly blows Zomo and Aku off the top of the grave. "Murder!" he roars.

"Help!! Rescue!!! Let me out of here. It's all a mistake. Don't be angry, Kura. I'll explain everything."

"Gggrrr, Snap-crunch, Gggrrr," goes Aku, while Zomo goes on scrabbling harder than ever.

"Stop!" shouts Bunsuru. "Pax!! Mercy!!! If you let me off, Kura, I'll give you the five thousand I owe Zomo."

Scrabble, scrabble, scrabble goes Zomo.

"Ten thousand then," cries Bunsuru.

"Gggrrr, Snap-crunch, Gggrrr," goes Aku.

"All right, fifteen thousand," roars Bunsuru.

Scrabble, scrabble, scrabble goes Zomo, and *"Gggrrr, Snap-crunch, Gggrrr,"* goes Aku.

"Very well then—twenty thousand," bellows old Bunsuru in desperation.

At this Zomo and Aku stop and stand aside. Bunsuru now begins working from the inside, and by and by he makes an opening in the roof of the grave and pops up through it like a jack-in-the-box. And

mighty surprised he is, to find Zomo and Aku standing there in the moonlight when he is expecting Kura.

"Where is Kura?" he asks as soon as he gets his breath back.

"He cannot wait," says Zomo, "so he leaves us here to collect the money you promise."

Bunsuru looks as though he is going to say something, but he thinks better of it. Instead he takes Zomo and Aku over to the house and counts out twenty thousand in cash.

"What is that for?" asks the nanny when Zomo and Aku have gone.

"Listening to a woman's advice," says Bunsuru, looking sour enough to curdle the milk.

"It is not my advice you listen to," says the nanny huffily. "It is that old fool of a camel's."

"Well, whoever's it is," says Bunsuru, "it costs me twenty thousand."

When the news of what happens to Bunsuru reaches Rakumi the Camel, he bursts out laughing. "Poor old Bunsuru," he says, "twenty thousand, did you say? Well, it doesn't surprise me. You have to be smart to get the better of that Zomo."

From the way he says this, you can see that he fancies that he is the one to do the trick.

Shorty -the- Bow

THE SCORPION's real name is Kunama, but he likes to be called Shorty-the-Bow because he says it is his family title.

One night, when the moon is shining so bright that Jemage the Fruit-bat complains of the glare and will not budge from his house, Shorty-the-Bow is walking along, minding his own business, when he hears footsteps coming up behind him in the sand—*Ker-runch, Ker-runch, Ker-runch.* Now Shorty knows that some of his neighbors can be mighty careless about where they put their feet, especially Rakumi the Camel who has feet as big as millstones, and so when he hears this crunching coming up behind him he shouts, "Mind your step," and brings his tail to readiness.

But it is not Rakumi the Camel who is coming up behind Shorty, it is Kura the Hyena. He does not hear Shorty's shout, on account of Shorty's voice being no more than a squeak at the best of times, but as he is hunting for his dinner he has his muzzle close to the ground and so luckily he sees Shorty before he steps on him.

"Hey, you!" he sings out, treating Shorty very cavalier. "You ought to carry a light at night, you ought, or you'll get trodden on."

Now if there is one thing that rubs Shorty up the wrong way, it is being treated cavalier by people like hyenas. So he turns round, and he looks Kura up and down, and he hitches his tail a bit higher, and then, very cool, he says, "Are you speaking to me?"

"Of course, I'm speaking to you," says Kura. "Who else?"

"In that case" says Shorty "I will trouble you to address me by my name or title."

"I know that Zaki the Lion has a title," says Kura, "and I hear that some people address Dila the Jackal as Clerk of the Bush, but I am never told that anyone ever calls you by any title. Furthermore," he goes on, "seeing as how you are so short that you cannot even see over my big toe, I am wondering how you ever come to have a title at all."

"It comes to me," says Shorty, "from my father

and my grandfather and my great-grandfather."

"Oh?" says Kura. "And what is this title that comes to you from your father and your grandfather and your great-grandfather?"

"It is Shorty-the-Bow," says Shorty.

"Now you mention it," says Kura. "I hear people call you Shorty-the-Bow, but I think you are joking because I never see you shoot anything in my life. Tell me," he goes on, "what sort of game can you shoot?"

"Large or small," says Shorty, "it makes no difference to me."

"Well, do you know what I think?" says Kura. "I think you're a braggart, and I don't believe that you've ever shot anything bigger than a field-mouse."

"No?" says Shorty.

"No," says Kura.

"All right," says Shorty, "just you try me out and see."

"I'll do that," says Kura. "Come along with me, and I'll give you something to shoot at." So saying, he sets off towards the palace, and Shorty follows along behind as fast as he can go, which is not very fast on account of his legs being so short.

It is the hot weather, and so when Kura and Shorty reach the palace, they find that Zaki the Lion is holding court in the open. Giwa the Elephant is there with his wife, and Bauna the Bush-cow is there with her husband, and Damisa the Leopard, and

Rakumi the Camel, and Biri the Monkey, and fifty others great and small. The throne has been brought out of the palace, and Zaki is sitting there, with all the other animals gathered around him in a circle, and they are all being mighty respectful and saying, "God give the Chief long life," and "Yes, Lords of the Bush," and "No, Lords of the Bush," and such things to show what loyal subjects they are.

Kura leads the way towards the edge of the circle, but he stops short before he gets there so that the lion will not see him and the others will not hear what he wishes to say.

"Now then," he says, turning to Shorty, "do you see Zaki over there?"

"Of course I see Zaki over there," says Shorty.

"Well then," says Kura, "if you are such a good shot, just you take out your bow and knock him off

his throne, and then I'll believe you."

When Kura says this, he doesn't for a moment think that Shorty will take up his challenge, and so he is very surprised when Shorty says that this target will suit him down to the ground. "There's just one thing though," Shorty goes on, "my bow's uncommon whippy, and so I may need your help while I'm bending it."

"What do you want me to do?" asks Kura, who still thinks that Shorty is bragging.

"Just bring your nose down here," says Shorty, "and hold me steady."

"Like this?" asks Kura.

"Closer," says Shorty. "I need to brace myself on account of my bow being so whippy."

"How's this?" says Kura.

"Closer," says Shorty.

"How's this now?" says Kura.

"That's fine," says Shorty. "Now hold tight because this bow of mine has a mighty powerful backlash."

"Seeing is believing," says Kura, who still thinks that Shorty can no more shoot than fly.

"Well, don't say I didn't warn you," says Shorty.

"Stop bragging and start shooting," says Kura.

"All right," says Shorty. "Here goes."

Now all this time Kura's muzzle is resting on Shorty's tail. When he says, "Here goes," Shorty takes his sting and plunges it into Kura's snout until it won't go any further, and then he gives it a twist or two for good measure.

If Kura has any friends, which he hasn't, they will not claim that he is a man of many feelings. But what feelings he has are right there at the end of his snout, and so when Shorty's sting goes in, and it loaded with Shorty's best brand of poison, which he brews himself, Kura jumps about eight feet in the air and turns two and a half somersaults and lands back on his head and knocks himself clean out.

Now Kura does not know it, but while he is cart-wheeling about in the air, he is also letting out a bellow such as the other creatures have never heard before and say afterwards that they never wish to hear again. This surprises them so much, that they do not wait to see what is going on but with one accord they spring onto their four feet and take off in whichever direction they happen to be pointing at the time.

Zaki the Lion is no better than the rest of them. As a rule he doesn't like people to see him hurrying, because he thinks that it isn't dignified, but this time he forgets his dignity and goes galloping off with the best of them so that before long he is way out in front of the field.

Giwa the Elephant also forgets about his dignity and is in such a hurry to get out of there that he bumps into the giraffe and bowls him over. Furthermore, he is so careless about where he puts his feet, that it is a great mercy that he doesn't trample anyone to death.

As for the giraffe, he lies on the ground after

Giwa has bowled him over, and half-a-dozen other creatures who are in a hurry to get away trip over that long neck of his. When they bite the dust, they bring down another dozen who are coming along behind, and so for a time there is great confusion and hubbub on all sides.

Shorty waits until the hullabaloo dies down, and then he goes over to the throne where Zaki the Lion has been sitting and climbs up and makes himself comfortable.

By and by Kura comes round and sits up and

rubs his head. He does not know what has happened to him and so he is surprised to find a bump on his skull as big as the eggs which the wife of Jimina the Ostrich lays, if not bigger. And when he looks round to see what has become of all the other animals, he is even more surprised to find that there is not a single one in sight, when just now there have been fifty or more.

"Shorty," he cries, "where have you got to?"

"There is no need to shout," says Shorty. "I'm over here."

Kura cannot see him at first, but he goes over to the throne, which is where Shorty's voice comes from, and when he finds him sitting up there, as cool as a cucumber, he is so surprised that you can knock him over with a feather.

Kura does not take any more chances with Shorty but begins to treat him as polite as you please. After this it is, "Yes, Shorty-the-Bow," and "No, Shorty-the-Bow," and every now and again he thinks that maybe there is no harm in throwing in a "God give you long life" as well, just to be on the safe side.

Saddle
and
Spurs

ONE DAY Kura the Hyena is walking along the road when he meets a Mallam, or learned man, riding a horse. The Mallam is old and thin, and he has a white beard that reminds Kura of Bunsuru the Billy-goat. The horse has stopped in the middle of a clearing in the bush, and the man is trying to make him go again.

If the man looks old, the horse looks older still. His ribs stand out, and his head is hanging down so far that his muzzle is almost touching the ground.

"There's not much meat on the carcass," thinks Kura to himself, "but there may be some nice marrow in those bones."

Now usually when it comes to men, Kura is not one to push himself forward because men are the friends of Kare the Dog, and Kare the Dog is no friend of Kura's. But with this man it is different because he carries no spear or sword and is so thin that it looks as if a good puff will blow him over. So Kura marches up to him as bold as brass and asks where he comes from and where he is bound for.

The Mallam does not see Kura come up and starts so much when he hears him speak that he nearly falls off his horse with surprise. When he recovers, he says that he comes from Yabo and is a pilgrim bound for Mecca.

"Well, what's amiss then?" asks Kura.

"It's my horse," says the Mallam. "He is old and will not go."

"Then I will make a bargain with you," says Kura.

"What sort of bargain?" asks the Mallam, who in his day has heard a lot about hyenas and none of it good.

"I long have a fancy to own a riding horse of my own," says Kura, "and if you let me have this one, I will take you to Mecca myself."

"Do you mean to say," asks the Mallam, "that you will let me ride you to Mecca and back?" He is beginning to think that hyenas are by no means as bad as they are painted.

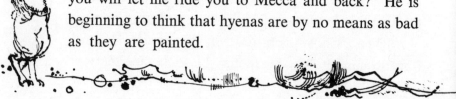

"That's right," says Kura, looking as amiable as
he can, which most people do not find any more amiable than a man-trap.

"Mark you," he goes on, "I will not do the same
for everyone. But you are a learned and pious man, and
I see you set your heart on going to Mecca, and so I
will do it for you as a favor."

Just at this moment, who should come walking
past but Zomo the Rabbit. Kura looks at him as if he

was a stink-bug in the stewpot, but the Mallam calls him over to be a witness to the bargain. When it is explained to Zomo, he wonders what Kura is up to, because he knows that he never has a riding horse that does not finish up in his larder, but he keeps mum and asks no questions.

After the bargain is struck, and Zomo has gone his way, Kura tells the Mallam that he will just take the horse home and then he will come back and pick him up and carry him to Mecca.

"I won't be long," he says, "so wait here till I get back." With this he goes off with the horse, and the Mallam spreads out his saddlecloth on the ground and settles down to wait.

As soon as Kura is out of sight of the Mallam, he starts laughing, and he laughs and laughs until the tears run down his cheeks. "Rich," he says to himself. "I take his horse, and he thinks I do him a favor. Zomo's not the only smart one around here."

When he gets home, his old woman runs her eye over the horse. "He's very skinny," she says, "but his bones look good."

"That's just what I think," says Kura. "Feed him up for a couple of days, and he'll do well enough."

Two days later Zomo comes back from visiting his relations, and when he reaches the clearing, he finds the Mallam still sitting on his saddlecloth.

"If it's Kura you're waiting for," he says, "you'll be waiting a long time."

"Won't he come back then?" asks the Mallam.

"Not he," says Zomo. "If he has not already eaten that horse of yours, then I will bet that he is fattening him up for dinner today."

"Alas and alack!" says the Mallam, "Now I shall never get to Mecca." So saying, he begins to wail and beat his brow.

When Zomo sees this, he feels sorry for the old man. "I'll tell you what," he says, "if your horse is still alive, I'll get him back for you." With this he takes the saddle, bridle, and spurs and tells the Mallam to go and hide by the silk-cotton tree and wait till he comes.

So the Mallam sets off for the silk-cotton tree, which is down towards the river. As for Zomo, he throws the saddle and bridle over his shoulder, puts the spurs in his pocket, and takes the road that leads to the hyena's house. After a bit he stops and puts the bridle down at the side of the path. Later on he stops again and puts the saddle down. Then, when he comes in sight of the house, he begins to hobble as if he is lame.

"Are you there, Kura?" he sings out when he reaches the hyena's gate.

Now Kura has taught his children that if anyone comes asking for him at the house, they are always to say that he is out. So when they hear Zomo outside, they shout and say, "He's not here."

"What a pity!" says Zomo. "Anyway, tell him that I have been here looking for him."

"All right," says the eldest cub. "Do you wish to

leave a message?"

"Never mind," says Zomo. "It's just that I know where there's some meat, but I expect those vultures will finish it off before Kura gets back."

As soon as he hears the word *meat,* old Kura, who all this time is at the back of the house, pricks up his ears and shouts, "Who is it?"

"It's Zomo," the cubs shout back, "and he says he knows where there's some meat."

"Tell him to wait then," says Kura, and next minute he pops out from where he has been hiding.

"Glad to see you," says Zomo. "Your family say you are out."

"Boobies!" Kura shouts at the cubs. "Blockheads!! Blunderbusses!!! What do you mean by saying I'm out when I'm in?"

"But Baba," says the eldest cub, "you tell us . . ."

"Silence!" roars Kura. "Not another word. Now Zomo," he goes on, "what is this I hear about meat?"

"That's right," says Zomo. "Not far from here either, but we shall have to hurry."

"What are we waiting for then?" says Kura. "Let's go."

Zomo and Kura set off together and head towards the river. Zomo is still hobbling, and so Kura keeps getting ahead of him and having to wait.

"What's the matter with you today?" he asks. "Can't you go any faster?"

"I sprained my ankle," says Zomo.

"That's very annoying of you," says Kura. "Just

when we're in a hurry."

"I can't help it," says Zomo.

"Here, I know," says Kura. "Hop up on my back, and I'll carry you."

"But I shall fall off," says Zomo.

"No you won't," says Kura. "Not if you hold on tight."

So Zomo gets up on Kura's back, and they set off again.

"Kura," he says when they have gone a little way, "your fur is tickling me."

"I can't help that," says Kura.

Just then they pass the Mallam's saddle, which is still lying at the side of the road. "Wait a bit, Kura," says Zomo. "If we put this thing on your back and I sit on it, I shall be all right."

"Oh, very well then," says Kura. "But hurry."

So Zomo dismounts and puts the saddle on Kura's back and does up the girths. "There, that's better," he says. "We shall get on faster now."

Kura is going along at a trot with Zomo on his back when Angulu the Vulture flies past. "There, did you see him?" cries Zomo. "It's Angulu, making for our meat."

When he hears this, Kura breaks into a canter. "Help," cries Zomo, throwing his arms round Kura's neck. "I'm falling off."

"I can't help that," says Kura. "I'm not going to let Angulu get all that meat."

Just then they pass the bridle, which is lying by

the side of the path where Zomo has put it. "Wait a minute," says Zomo. "If we tie this thing over your head, I shall be able to hold on to it, and then we can really go fast."

"Oh, very well," says Kura. "But do be quick."

So Zomo dismounts again and puts the bridle over Kura's head and fastens it. Then he remounts, and they set off once more.

As they are cantering along, Zomo takes the spurs out of his pocket and starts putting them on. "Hey Zomo," says Kura, "what are you doing up there?"

"My ankle's hurting," says Zomo, "and I'm rubbing it."

When he's ready, Zomo lifts his left leg and digs the spur into Kura's flank with all his might.

"Ouch!" bellows Kura and breaks into a gallop.

"What's wrong with you?" asks Zomo.

"I'm not sure," says Kura, "but I think a hornet stung me."

Before long Kura begins to puff and blow with all the running he is doing, and so Zomo lifts his right leg and drives the spur into his other flank.

"Yaroo!" bellows Kura and breaks into a gallop again.

"What's wrong now?" asks Zomo.

"I don't know," says Kura, "but I think a scorpion stung me."

"Nonsense!" says Zomo. "How can a scorpion sting you up there? It's your imagination."

By now Kura is puffing and blowing fit to bust, but each time he tries to slow down, Zomo gives him another dig with the spurs. When they reach the silk-cotton tree, he pulls on the reins and by this time Kura is glad enough of a rest. But as soon as he stops, the Mallam pops out from behind the trunk and slips the halter over his head. So before Kura knows what is happening, he finds himself a prisoner.

Well, there's not much more to tell. Zomo goes back and breaks the news to Kura's old woman that if she ever wants to see her husband again she must hand over the Mallam's horse. The horse has put on quite a bit of flesh by this time, and so at first Kura's wife doesn't want to give him up, but when Zomo tells her that the Mallam has Kura saddled and bridled and ready to ride to Mecca—why then she just goes to the stables and brings the horse out and hands him over.

As for the old Mallam, when he sees his horse again, he is so pleased that he says he doesn't know how he can ever repay Zomo. Zomo says he doesn't want any payment, but he has a favor to ask just the same.

"What is it?" asks the Mallam.

"Why this," says Zomo, "just keep old Fouljowl there tied up until I'm out of sight."

So saying, he looks down at his own two feet. "Feet," he says to them, "what have I ever had that I didn't share with you?"

With this, he takes off so fast that he showers the Mallam with gravel, and before you can say "Jack Robinson" he has skedaddled into the bush and vanished.

Double
or
Quits

WHEN THEY SEE what happens to Bunsuru the Billy-goat, most of the animals who still owe Zomo money pay up before worse things befall. But not Rakumi the Camel. He goes about telling his friends that others can do as they please, but that for his part he does not mean to pay a penny, much less five thousand. Very haughty about it he is, too, so that all the animals say that he must have a trick up his sleeve.

Well, so long as Zomo is in funds, he doesn't bother about Rakumi's debt, but when his cash begins to run short, he thinks he'll drop a hint. And so next time he's up that way, he calls at the camel's house.

When Zomo first mentions the five thousand, Rakumi pretends that he doesn't know what the talk is all about. Then when Zomo reminds him about Damisa the Leopard, he says that it is such a small matter that it quite slips his mind. "Now that you mention it," he goes on, "of course it comes back to me, but I can't pay you just now because I have no small change in my pocket." Zomo says he is in no hurry and tomorrow will do.

The next time that Zomo mentions this debt, Rakumi sounds quite huffy. "To a man of the world like me," he says, "five thousand is just chicken feed." He gives Zomo to understand that a camel can't be expected to remember such a trifle and that furthermore he doesn't consider it very gentlemanly of Zomo to keep raking it up.

The third time that Zomo asks for his money, Rakumi pretends to have an idea. "Look," he says, "five thousand is not worth quarreling about, so I'll tell you what we'll do. We'll have a bet for double or quits."

"What do you wish to bet about?" asks Zomo.

"Let's see," says Rakumi, as if he is trying to think of something on the spur of the moment, though actually it is all worked out beforehand. "I know," he goes on like a man who suddenly has an idea. "I bet you can't get a bag of corn from a farmer." He lays this bet because of course he knows that getting corn out of a farmer is like getting blood out of a locust.

"Very well then," says Zomo. "Double or quits on

five thousand."

Next day Zomo goes and hides in the grass beside the path that men use when they are going to their market. He waits until he sees a pagan coming along with a bag of corn on his head, and then he comes out of the grass and lies down at the side of the path. He lies there as if dead with his mouth open and his teeth bared. When the farmer comes up, he stops and turns Zomo over with his foot. "That's funny," he says to himself, "he's still quite warm." With this he passes on.

As soon as his back is turned, Zomo jumps up and doubles round ahead of him. Then he lies down in the path and again pretends to be dead. When the farmer comes up, he stops and stares at Zomo. "That's very funny," he says to himself. "I wonder what's killing all these rabbits." So saying he goes on again.

As soon as his back is turned, Zomo doubles round ahead of him again. This times he lies down in the path near a tree stump. When the farmer comes up and sees him there, he says to himself, "This is too good to miss. If I go back and pick up those other two rabbits, I'll have three, and they'll fetch fifteen hundred any day." So saying, he puts his bag of corn down on the tree stump and hurries back up the path.

As soon as the farmer is out of sight, Zomo jumps up, humps the bag of corn onto his back, and scuttles off into the bush. Then he makes his way to the camel's house and puts his load down at the gate. "Rakumi," he sings out, "I've got something to show you."

The camel's face falls when he comes out and sees

the bag. "Oh, all right," he says when he has opened it and looked inside. "You win."

"That's ten thousand then," says Zomo.

"I'll lay you another bet," says the camel.

"All right," says Zomo. "What is it this time?"

"I'll bet you double or quits," says the camel, "that you can't bring me a calabash full of milk."

"What's so difficult about that?" asks Zomo.

"Wait till you hear," says the camel looking very artful. "I don't want just any old milk. I want the bush-cow's milk."

"Very well then," says Zomo. "Double or quits on ten thousand for a calabash full of the bush-cow's milk."

For the rest of the afternoon Zomo sits in the shade of the *chediya* tree with his thinking cap on. Sometimes he thinks so hard that he closes his eyes and seems to be breathing very deep, but at supper that night he is as lively as ever.

Early next morning he takes a large calabash from the pantry and goes off in search of the bandicoot. "Gafiya," he says when he finds him, "will you do me a good turn?"

"What's in it for me?" asks Gafiya.

"A fifth share," says Zomo.

"On how much?" asks Gafiya, who is no fool.

"On ten thousand," says Zomo.

"Done," says Gafiya. "What do you want me to do?"

"It's quite simple," says Zomo. "I want you to

come along with me, and each time I say, 'I tell you she can,' you must say, 'I tell you she can't.' "

"That sounds easy enough," says Gafiya.

So Zomo and Gafiya set off together in search of the bush-cow. They find her far away in the bush where she has a field of hay that she is thinking of cutting. "I tell you she can," says Zomo in a loud voice as soon as they spot her.

"I tell you she can't," says Gafiya.

"I tell you she can," says Zomo.

"I tell you she can't," says Gafiya.

The bush-cow hears them talking and looks up. "Oh, hello Bauna," says Zomo, as if he is surprised to see her. "Fancy meeting you here!"

"Are you looking for me?" asks the bush-cow.

"Oh, no," says Zomo. "We just happen to be talking about you, that's all."

"And what are you saying?" asks the bush-cow, not looking at all pleased.

"As a matter of fact," says Zomo, "we are having an argument. I am saying that you are so strong that if you want you can split any tree in the bush from top to bottom."

"That's right," says the bush-cow. "And what is Gafiya saying?"

With this she glares so hard at the bandicoot that he begins to wish that he had not come.

"Well," says Zomo, "Gafiya here doesn't think you can. That's right, isn't it Gafiya?"

"No," says Gafiya, looking more nervous than

ever. "I mean yes."

"Oh, you don't, don't you?" says the bush-cow, looking about as matronly as a two-handed battle-ax. "We'll have to see about that. You go and find the biggest tree you like, and I'll split it right down the middle for you."

So they all three of them go off and find a baobab tree that is so broad in the trunk that even Giwa the Elephant can hide behind it if he likes and you will not notice him.

"It's very big," says Zomo, as if he is not sure whether even the bush-cow can split such a tree.

"Fiddlesticks!" says Bauna. "I can manage this all right."

"Well, you must take a good run at it then," says Zomo. "Here—let me clear a path for you."

So the bush-cow waits while Zomo and Gafiya clear a runway for her. When they have finished, she goes up to the far end and swings round to face the baobab. "Now watch," she tells them. Then she paws the ground once or twice, lowers her head, and charges. She comes thundering along the path with her head down and tail up, faster and faster, until she hits the tree—*Ker-rash*.

As soon as the splinters have stopped flying and the dust has settled, Zomo and Gafiya hurry forward. They find the bush-cow standing there with her horns buried deep in the trunk of the tree and her eyes closed.

"Quick, the calabash," says Zomo and starts milking her where she stands.

When Bauna comes to her senses again, she finds the bandicoot standing by to set her free, but there is no sign of Zomo because by this time he is halfway home with the milk.

Rakumi the Camel looks very suspicious when Zomo gets back, and at first he refuses to believe that the milk is the bush-cow's. But by and by the bandicoot joins them, and then he has to agree that Zomo has won the bet. "All right," he says. "So I owe you twenty thousand—what of it?"

This same night Rakumi is biting his nails over the bets he has lost when an idea comes to him. So he goes over to the bandicoot's house and asks how Zomo managed to get the bush-cow's milk. When Gafiya has told him the whole story, Rakumi says that Zomo is not the only one who can play this game.

Next morning Zomo is sitting outside his house after breakfast, wondering how to spend the money that the camel owes him, when who should appear but the camel himself.

"Hullo, Rakumi," he says. "I wasn't expecting you so soon. If you wish to pay me a thousand or two on account, I will not say no."

"I am not coming to pay anything," says Rakumi. "I am coming to lay you another bet."

"All right," says Zomo. "What do you wish to bet on now?"

"I have had to think of all the bets so far," says Rakumi. "This time it's your turn."

"But there's nothing I want to bet on," says Zomo.

"Well, how about this?" says the camel. "Bet me that I can't put Kumurchi the Black Cobra into a satchel and deliver him here to your door before sunset?"

"All right," says Zomo. "How much?"

"Twenty thousand," says Rakumi. "Double or quits."

"Done," says Zomo.

The giraffe and the roan-antelope are called in as

witnesses. When they have taken up their positions, the camel stalks off, and they sit down under the *chediya* tree to wait.

First the camel collects a leather satchel from his house and then he goes in search of the bandicoot. "Gafiya," he says when he finds him, "I want you to come and help me."

"How?" asks the bandicoot.

"It's quite simple," says the camel. "All you have to do is to come along with me, and when I say, 'I tell you he'll fill it,' you must say, 'I tell you he won't.' "

"All right," says the bandicoot, "what's my share?"

"A tenth," says the camel.

"Only a tenth?" says the bandicoot. "Zomo gives me a fifth."

"I can't help what Zomo gives you," snaps the camel. "I'm offering you a tenth."

"And I'm refusing," says the bandicoot.

"Out of my way, serf," says the camel. "I never haggle with my inferiors." With this, he stalks away and goes in search of the black cobra by himself.

The cobra is sunning himself in the grass when the camel arrives. Rakumi doesn't notice him at first but goes blundering about the compound saying, "I tell you he'll fill it," and, "I tell you he won't." Kumurchi watches him for a bit and then he suddenly raises his head and says, "Who are you looking for?"

This makes the camel jump. "Oh, there you are, Kumurchi," he says. "Fancy meeting you here."

"I live here," says Kumurchi, "so it's not surprising that you meet me here."

"Oh, yes of course you do," says the camel, who is beginning to get confused.

"Are you looking for me?" asks the cobra.

"No, not looking for you," says the camel. "Gafiya and I are just talking about you, that's all."

"But Gafiya isn't here," says the cobra.

"Oh, no, nor he is," says the camel, who is now getting rattled because the cobra stares at him so coldly. "I am forgetting."

"I've been watching you for some time," says the cobra, "and you've been acting in a very suspicious way." As he says this, he lifts his head higher, spreads out his hood, and begins to edge forward toward the camel, looking very nasty.

"Now, now," says the camel, backing away. "Don't be angry."

"Why shouldn't I be angry if I want to be?" says the

cobra. "What are you doing on my land anyway?"

"Oh, nothing, nothing," says the camel, backing away again.

All this time the cobra is swaying his head from side to side as if he is making sure that his machinery is in good working order. "And what's in that satchel of yours?" he asks moving forward again.

"Nothing," says the camel, backing away once more. "Nothing at all."

"Just as I thought," says the cobra. "It's my belief that you have come here to steal the eggs that my wife lays."

At this, the camel does not wait for more, but turns tail and bolts.

Back in town Zomo is sitting in the shade, talking to the giraffe and the roan-antelope, when suddenly there is a loud commotion. They all stop to listen, and in the distance they hear the camel shouting "Pax" and "Help" and "Rescue" and "Murder." Next minute he comes round the corner with his neck stretched out straight in front of him, shambling along so fast that it looks as if his hind legs are trying to overtake his front legs. And there, right behind him, comes the cobra,

snapping at his heels as if he wishes to have trotters for dinner.

As they go past Zomo's house, the cobra is shouting, "I'll teach you to steal my eggs, you splay-footed slobbergob," and "Just wait till I catch you, you hump-rumped hornswoggler." As for the camel, he has no more breath for hollering but his legs are working so fast to keep him ahead of the cobra that you will think he is practicing for the centipedes' ball. When they disappear over the hill, they are still going strong, and there is no need for the witnesses to wait till sunset to say that Zomo is the winner of the bet and that Rakumi now owes him forty thousand.

Well, this is the last bet the camel lays for a long time to come. The funny thing is that the one who seems most pleased is not Zomo, as you will expect, but Bunsuru the Billy-goat. "Forty thousand," he says and fairly cackles with laughter. When he is asked what is so funny, he says, "Can't you see? This makes Rakumi twice as big a fool as I."

Treasure Trove

ONE DAY Zomo is called away from home because his father's youngest brother is sick and his aunt thinks that he will die. His uncle lives on the far side of the Gundumi Bush, and it takes Zomo two days to reach the bedside. But when he gets there, the bed is empty because his uncle disappoints his heirs by recovering. Zomo spends three days with his uncle and aunt and then gets ready to return home.

Now the Gundumi Bush is very large and very sandy. What is more, on account of there being no water except in two wells, it is also very empty. No one

lives there, and not many people even try to cross it
because it is safer as well as more comfortable to go
the long way round.

But Zomo knows the short cut, and so he fills his
water bottle and sets off from his uncle's house. By the
time he reaches the second of the two wells, the sun
is already starting to sink and his water is nearly finished. This doesn't worry him until he goes to fill his
water bottle, and then he finds that the well is dry.

Now, although Zomo does not know it, this well
has been dry for some time, and it happens that rob-
bers have been using it to hide the stuff that they take
from merchants crossing the bush. It is almost dark
inside, and when Zomo first looks down he does not see

anything; but when he looks again to make sure that there is no water, he is surprised to find that the well is half full of bales and baskets.

By the time Zomo reaches home, he is feeling very tired and thirsty, but he does not mind this because he is thinking about the treasure. All that worries him now is how to lay his hands on it before someone else comes along.

Next day, Zomo sits out under his *chediya* tree with his thinking cap on and thinks and thinks. He does not wish to tell his friends what he knows because he will not trust them with a penny round the corner, let alone buried treasure. Try as he will, though, he can't think of any way of getting the stuff out of the well by himself, and so in the end he decides to ask Biri the Monkey to help him. In point of fact, he doesn't trust him any more than the others and the only reason he chooses him is on account of his being such a handy-man with his feet.

So in the evening Zomo goes off and calls on Biri. "Biri," he says when they have exchanged greetings, "I have a proposition to put to you."

"What is it?" asks Biri.

"I've found some treasure," says Zomo, "and I want you to help me get it."

"And if I do," says Biri, "what's in it for me?"

"A fifth," says Zomo.

Biri shakes his head.

"A quarter then," says Zomo.

"Not enough," says Biri.

"All right," says Zomo, "a third, and that's my last word."

"Fair enough," says Biri. "When do we start?"

"Tomorrow," says Zomo. "Meet me at my house and bring a water bottle with you."

"Very well," says Biri. "I'll be there."

When Zomo and Biri set off next morning, they both carry water bottles, and Zomo also has a coil of rope. It is nearly noon before they reach the well, and they are glad to find that the treasure is still lying down there at the bottom.

"Now then," says Zomo, "one of us must go down the well while I stay here to haul the stuff out."

"I'm not afraid of work," says Biri, who never does a hand's turn if he can possibly avoid it. "You go down, and I'll stay here and haul."

"No, you go down," says Zomo, "and let me haul."

"No, no," says Biri. "You aren't strong enough to haul up these big bales. Besides," he adds, "if I go down perhaps you aren't strong enough to haul me up either."

Zomo is by no means eager to go down the well, but he sees that Biri will not budge and so he has to agree. When he reaches the bottom, he ties the end of the rope to the first bale, and Biri hauls it up to the top.

"Hold on," says Biri as he unties the rope. "Let me move this bale clear or otherwise we shall get cluttered up round here."

So saying, he picks up the bale and carries it away

from the well and puts it down behind some bushes. The reason he does this is that he thinks he will out-smart Zomo. When he has put the bale down behind the bushes, he looks about for a large stone. The one that he finds is as big as Kura the Hyena's head and twice as heavy, and he picks it up and carries it back to the well. He is careful not to let Zomo know what he is doing, though, and so he puts the stone down where it is out of sight.

When the second bale comes up, Biri carries it away and puts it beside the first one. Then he finds another big stone and takes it back to the well. When the third bale comes up, he does the same thing again.

Biri and Zomo go on working like this, and the stack of bales behind the bushes grows bigger and bigger. So, too, does the pile of stones at the top of the well. Since Biri takes so long to stack each bale, Zomo guesses that he is up to something, and he is sure that it is no good, but he doesn't know what it is.

The sun is beginning to sink before they get down to the bottom of the bales and baskets in the well.

"How many more?" asks Biri.

"Only three," says Zomo. "Two little ones and then a big one to finish up with. After that there is only me."

"We mustn't forget you, must we?" says Biri. "That will never do."

Zomo is not sure that he likes the way Biri says this. So while Biri is carrying away the smaller bales, Zomo makes a hole in the big one, which is to go up last. By and by, Biri comes back and throws the rope down again. Zomo makes it fast to the big bale, and then he jumps into the hole he has made. Luckily for him, it is so dark by this time that Biri can't see what he is doing down there. When Zomo has hidden himself in the bale, he sticks his head out and shouts, "You can haul away now, Biri, and then come back for me."

Up at the top Biri shakes with laughing when he hears Zomo say he can come back for him. "Don't worry," he shouts as he hauls the bale up. "I'll be back, and I shall have a surprise for you."

When Biri carries the last bale over to the stack behind the bushes, he doesn't know that Zomo is inside. He puts the bale down and then goes to look for another stone to take back to the well. He finds a rock that is as big as Zaki the Lion's head and so heavy that he can hardly carry it. As he staggers off toward the well, Zomo creeps out of the bale in which he is hiding to see what is going on.

When Biri gets back to the well, he is looking as mean as a parcel of misers. "Mind your head, Zomo," he sings out. "Rope coming down now." With this, he heaves the rock into the well and stands there listening. The rock goes down the shaft of the well and hits the bottom with an almighty *Ker-boomph*. When he hears this, Biri cackles with laughter as if it is the funniest joke he's ever played.

"I tell you to mind your head, Zomo," he shouts, but there is no answer.

"Are you still there, Zomo?" he shouts again. Still no answer.

"I don't trust that Zomo," he says out loud, and with that he starts picking up the rest of the stones he has collected and pitching them into the well after the rock.

"Oho," says Zomo to himself when he sees what Biri is doing. "So this is how the land lies, is it? Well, two can play at this game." So saying, he goes back to where Biri has stacked the bales and baskets and cuts brushwood and covers them over so that they look like any other clump of bushes.

By and by, when Biri has thrown all his stones into the well, he comes back and starts looking for the bales. But it is dark by now and, since Zomo has covered them over, he can't find them anywhere. For a while he blunders about, stubbing his toes on tree stumps, and then he says to himself that there is no hurry anyway and that he will come back for the stuff in the morning when it is light.

After Biri has gone, Zomo uncovers the bales and baskets and sets to work. He empties all the goods that are in them and fills them up again with whatever rubbish he can find. When he has finished doing this, he hides the real merchandise in a place where he can fetch it later, but the bales he stacks out in the open where Biri will find them when he comes back.

Well, that is nearly the end of the story, but not quite. When Zomo gets home, he remembers that Rakumi the Camel still owes him ten thousand from the bets they have, and Rakumi agrees to fetch the merchandise for Zomo if he will cancel this debt. So Rakumi makes a couple of journeys and brings all the stuff to Zomo's doorstep. After this Zomo and his wife and children have more satin gowns and silk wraps and embroidered slippers than they ever possess before or since, not to mention cola-nuts, tobacco, and sherbet.

But with Biri it is a different story. He goes back and finds the bales and baskets that Zomo leaves for him; but he does not trust any of his friends to help him fetch them, and so he and his old woman keep sneaking off into the bush and bringing back a bale or a basket at a time. While they are doing this, he will not let her look inside; but he tells her that when they have fetched them all, they will be rich. It takes them ten days to bring in all the stuff, and it is so heavy that they both grow quite thin with work and worry.

When at last they get all the bales and baskets home, and are ready to open them, Biri goes round prodding them and telling his old woman what he thinks is in each one.

"By the look of it," he says, "this bale will be full of gowns and turbans. This one," he goes on, "feels like fezzes, and that one must be slippers. Embroidered slippers, I expect. This package smells like tobacco, and that basket is obviously cola-nuts."

But when they come to open them, they are disappointed; for where Biri says there are gowns and turbans, they see only bark and dried leaves, and where he says there are fezzes and slippers, they find only twigs and leaf-mold. As for the cola-nuts and tobacco, they turn out to be pebbles and toadstools.

This is bad enough, but what is worse is when Biri finds out that Zomo is not at the bottom of the well, but strutting about town with new clothes for every day of the week. Biri tries to keep out of Zomo's way, but one day he is taking the air with Gyado the Wart-

hog when they run into Zomo. He is wearing one of his new gowns and a pair of embroidered slippers from Timbuctoo and a turban of the best muslin, which is so big that when people see it in the distance they wonder whether maybe Angulu the Vulture has made a nest up there.

"My!" says Gyado to Zomo when they have greeted one another. "That's a mighty fine turban you're wearing today."

"Yes," says Zomo. "It's a pity that I wasn't wearing it the other day when something fell on my head." When he says this, Biri begins to look as if he wishes that he is somewhere else.

"What happened?" asks Gyado.

"Well, it's like this," says Zomo. "I am working at the bottom of a well and my friend who is helping me at the top dislodges a stone, which lands on my head and gives me a headache."

By this time Biri looks as if he will not mind if he is at the bottom of a well himself.

"Very careless of him," says Gyado.

"Yes," says Zomo. "If he was not my friend, I would suspect that he was trying to do me an injury." So saying, he looks very hard at Biri and asks him what he thinks.

But Biri still has no idea how Zomo escaped being flattened at the bottom of the well, and so he doesn't know where to look or what to say.

At this, Zomo gives out a loud cackle of laughter so that all the other animals stop and stare. They feel quite sorry for Biri, on account of his clothes looking so torn and tatty, and they wonder what trick Zomo has been up to this time to get hold of such a turban as even Zaki the Lion might be graciously pleased to wear.

A House
for the
Crocodile

No one knows who is the older, the elephant or the tortoise, because they can both remember times when the grandfathers and great-grandfathers and great-great-grandfathers of other animals were alive and walking about the earth. Aku the Parrot likes to make out that he is nearly as old as they are, but compared to them, he is just a boy and probably not a day over ninety. But some who pretend to know will tell you that Kada the Crocodile is probably the oldest of the whole lot. If length is anything to go by, he is certainly mighty old because he is just about as long as the giraffe is tall.

Until now, old Kada has always stayed in the water and minded his own business. This does not mean to say that he has a nice nature, of course, because no one will pretend that he has, even though he is popular with the birds on account of his lying on the sand with his mouth open and letting them pick his teeth for him. On the other hand, he is always quarreling with the hippo family, and the frogs and fishes do not have a good word to say for him. But until now, the land animals have no cause to complain.

It is Kada's sweet tooth that causes the trouble between him and Zaki the Lion. For years and years, Kada never realizes that he has a sweet tooth, and then one day, when he is strolling along the river bank in the hot weather, he takes a bite at a stick of sugar cane and everything changes for him.

From now on, he has no appetite for his usual dishes. The big perch he has been trying to catch for the past year or more swims past under his nose and he pays no attention. The boys from the village come and bathe in his pool, and he doesn't go and look them over. Even when a fat market woman falls out of a canoe right above his head, he hardly bothers to look up. All he does is plague his old woman to make him sweet dishes and complain about the cooking if she gives him anything else.

Kada's wife now has to go to the market two or three times a week, and she finds this mighty troublesome because she doesn't like walking at the best of times. What makes matters worse is that she has to take up two baskets of fish to get the money to buy the sugar cane, and then she has to hump three bundles of cane all the way back to the river again. She soon gets tired of this caper, and one day she goes to her husband and says, "I've been thinking."

"What about?" says Kada.

"About saving money," says she.

"How can we do that?" asks Kada.

"I think it will be quite easy," says she. "The cane farms are right here on our doorstep, so why don't we just help ourselves?"

"Zaki the Lion will not like it if we do," says Kada. "They are in his territory."

"What can Zaki do to you?" she asks. "Anyway," she goes on, "if you want any more cane, you can fetch it yourself because I'm not going to that market again."

This puts old Kada in a fix because he knows that if he goes to the market himself and buys food, all the animals will say that his old woman has left him and will maybe laugh at him behind his back. Now Kada doesn't like to be laughed at, any more than Zaki the Lion or Giwa the Elephant, and furthermore his sweet tooth is giving him no peace. So gradually he comes round to the idea of going to the farms and getting his cane from there.

A day or two later, therefore, old Kada puts some money in his pocket and makes his way up to the river bank where the cane farms are. It is evening, and there is no one about so he lies down in the grass at the side of the path and waits.

By and by Jaki the Donkey appears with a big load of cane on his back. By this time it is beginning to get dark, and if there is one thing that Jaki dislikes it is darkness. In fact as he comes along, he is thinking about Kura the Hyena and cursing himself for staying out so late. The result is that when old Kada suddenly pops up out of the grass in front of him, he loses his head and panics.

"Murder!" he shouts and kicks up his heels to buck off his load. As soon as he is free of it, he takes off down the path as if he is a race horse and never pauses once until he is back by his own fireside.

Meanwhile, Kada picks up the cane and takes it home.

"How much was it?" asks his wife when he hands it over.

"I have no chance to pay," says Kada. "Jaki bolts before I can give him the money."

"Well, that's all right then," says his wife. "We get the cane free, and yet no one can say we steal it."

"It's funny that you say that," says Kada, "because the same idea comes to me, too."

This is the time of year when the animals are all cutting their cane, and during the next week or two Kada waylays Bunsuru the Billy-goat and Dila the Jackal. They both do what Jaki the Donkey has done and buck off their loads and take to their heels as fast as they can go. Neither of them has seen Kada on land before, and afterwards they say that his mouth is so big

that he can bite a horse in two if ever he needs to do so.

When Gyado the Warthog hears these tales, he is very scornful about them and calls it imagination. "Nothing," he says, "is going to stop me from getting my cane in." But when Kada jumps out at him that evening, he runs even faster than the others. Moreover, next day he goes about saying that he distinctly saw fire coming out of Kada's mouth and smoke pouring out of his nostrils.

After this there is nothing for it but to ask Zaki

the Lion for help. So next day Dila the Jackal and Jaki the Donkey and Bunsuru the Billy-goat put on their best gowns and go to the palace. The lion listens to what they have to say and then he asks them if they have any witnesses. When they say they have not, he tells them that they have no case and he cannot help them.

"But Lords of the Bush," says the Jackal, "Kada is plundering us."

"Well, what do you expect me to do?" asks the lion, who for once forgets to call himself by the royal plural.

It is not for nothing that Dila the Jackal has the title of Clerk of the Bush, which comes to him from his ancestors. "God give you long life," he says to the lion.

"Are you still our Chief or is Kada now ruler of the land as well as the water?"

This question needles the lion, which is what the jackal intends, and he says, "Oh, very well then, leave it to me."

Now the truth is that Zaki the Lion is in a quandary and doesn't at all know how to deal with the crocodile. First of all he tries sending the otter along with a message that he wants to see Kada in his palace at noon next day, but when the otter returns he says that he finds Kada very touchy.

"I give him your message," he tells the lion, "and when he hears it, he says things that I don't dare to repeat."

"Never fear," says the lion. "Tell us what he says."

"God give you long life," says the otter. "The first thing he says is that you may be the Chief up here, but he is the Chief down there."

"Go on," says the lion.

"And after that," the otter goes on, "he says, 'Since when has one Chief been able to send summonses to another Chief, who is as good as he, if not better?'"

"Oh, he says that, does he?" says the lion. "Go on."

"And after that," the otter goes on, "he says, 'You tell that moth-eaten old monarch of yours that I don't care a fig for any summons he sends me. You tell him that if he wants to meet me, he can come right down

to the water's edge because this is the boundary between his kingdom and my kingdom.' "

When they hear this, the other animals all tremble
in their shoes because they think that the lion will fly
into a rage and maybe take it out on them. But the lion
doesn't say anything because he is considering the
crocodile's proposition about meeting at the water's
edge. The more he thinks about it, the less he likes it.
He knows that he can't pull the crocodile out of the
water, but he has a nasty feeling that maybe the crocodile can pull him in.

Word now goes round among the animals that
Kada the Crocodile sends Zaki the Lion such an insult-
ing message that Zaki will have to teach him a lesson.
They wait for him to act, but nothing happens, and
they begin to grow restive. In the meantime old Kada
is going into the cane farms and helping himself to
whatever he wants. At this the animals grow very restive indeed, and voices are raised to ask what is the
good of having a Chief who is always taking tribute
from people but never protecting them when they need
it.

Now when Zomo hears all this talk, he has an
idea, and so he puts on his best gown and goes to the
palace to see the lion. He hears that Zaki has not slept
for three nights for thinking about Kada's message, and
when he is admitted to the audience chamber, he finds
Zaki grown quite thin with worry.

Well, the long and the short of it is that Zomo tells
the lion that he has a dodge or wheeze for putting the

crocodile in his place, and the lion says that if this wheeze or dodge comes off, he can ask for any reward he likes and he, the lion, will make it his personal business to see that he gets it.

Next day, Zomo goes and cuts some timber and collects creepers which will serve as rope. He hides these on one of the cane farms during the day, and in the evening he goes back and starts stacking them up as if they are a load of cane that he is going to take home.

While he is doing this, old Kada comes out of the water as usual and sees him working there. "Ho ho," he says to himself, "Zomo has a load of cane already cut. If I go and scare him off, it will save me the trouble of cutting more." So he creeps round behind Zomo and suddenly jumps out at him, thinking that he will make off like all the others.

But Zomo has been expecting him and doesn't seem at all surprised when he comes bouncing out. All he does is to look up and say, " 'Evening, Kada. How are you keeping?"

Kada is so taken aback at this that he doesn't know what to do, and so he says that he's pretty well, thank you, and hopes Zomo is the same.

Zomo says he's middling and can't complain.

After this, there is a silence, and Zomo gets on with his work. Kada feels awkward, standing there saying nothing; and so to make conversation, he asks Zomo what the timber is for, though he doesn't admit that he has just mistaken it for sugar cane.

"This?" says Zomo. "This is timber for a house that I'm going to build."

"Who for?" asks Kada.

"For Gyado the Warthog," says Zomo.

"Do you mean to say," asks Kada, "that on land even people like warthogs have houses?"

"Of course they do," says Zomo. "Don't tell me, Kada, that you haven't got a house of your own?"

Kada shakes his head and looks ashamed to admit that he doesn't have a house of his own.

"Well, you surprise me," says Zomo. "A great Chief like you and no house of your own! You really surprise me."

Kada stands and thinks for a while, and then he says, "Suppose you build a house for me, Zomo."

"I can't do that," says Zomo. "I promised Gyado that I will build one for him."

"Never mind about Gyado," says Kada. "You can build him one later."

Well, the long and the short of it is that old Kada is now so set on having a house of his own that he makes Zomo promise to build him one right there on the cane farm and to have it ready by the following evening.

Next morning, Zomo is up early, and he works on the house all through the day. He has to make it very long on account of the crocodile being so long himself, but he makes it very strong, too, and he anchors it firmly in the ground.

You and I, if we were to see this building of Zomo's, we might think that it looked more like a cage than a house. But old Kada, he has never seen a cage in his life, and so when he comes along in the evening, he thinks it is the finest house that ever is. "Zomo," he says, grinning all the way up his long snout, "you certainly make a good job of this house of mine."

"Glad you like it," says Zomo.

"Like it!" says Kada. "Why, I'll bet that even that lion of yours hasn't got a finer house than this."

"Well, why not go in and try it?" says Zomo. With this he opens the door, and old Kada waddles inside. When he's in there, Zomo shuts the door and slips a bar across and locks it. By and by, when Kada has seen all he wants to, he asks how he gets out.

"You don't," says Zomo.

"What do you say?" asks Kada, who thinks he does not hear aright.

"You don't," says Zomo. "You stay right there."

When old Kada finds that he is tricked, he starts kicking up an almighty rumpus. He tries bucking the

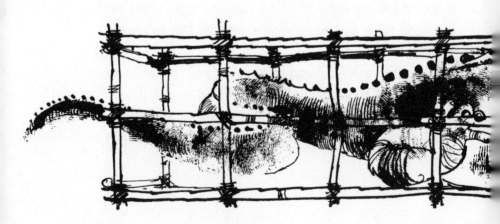

roof off, and he tries knocking the walls down with his tail, and then he tries burrowing down into the ground. It is none of it any good, though, because Zomo has made the cage too strong. When Kada finds he can't get out, he starts threatening Zomo with all the nasty things he will do to him and his family if he doesn't open the door. But Zomo pays no attention to this because he is building a fire near the cage.

When he is ready, Zomo sets a light to this fire, and it burns up very fierce. Kada doesn't like this one bit. By and by, when his skin gets hot through, he likes it even less because he begins to feel as if he is wearing a red hot suit of armor. This makes him change his tune and start hollering for mercy.

"Help!" he cries. But Zomo pays no attention and only goes off to get more wood.

"Have pity!" shouts Kada. "The fire's eating me." Zomo still pays no attention, but just throws a couple of logs on the fire.

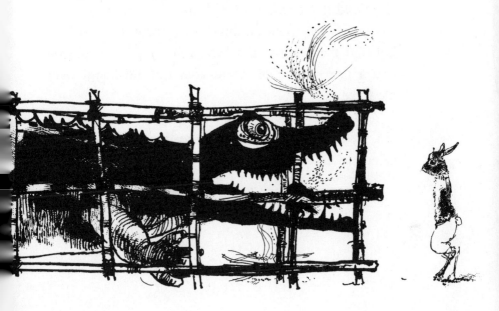

"I'll tell you what," says Kada, who is getting desperate, "if you'll let me go, I'll make you a present of my old woman. It's all her fault anyway."

"No," says Zomo. "You can keep your old woman; but if you promise one thing, I'll set you free."

By this time the fire is burning up fiercer than ever, and Kada is feeling about as happy as a pork chop at a barbecue. "I'll promise anything," he says, "so long as you let me out of here."

"All right," says Zomo. "If you promise to stick to the water and never come back on land, I'll let you go."

Kada's armor plating is now glowing all over, and his eyes are popping out of his head. He gives his promise, and so Zomo opens the door which faces the river and Kada comes out of the cage like a greyhound. In fact, the other animals who are watching say afterwards they never know he can get up on his toes like that and they are thankful that he is heading for the river and not coming after them.

Anyway, when he finally gets there, he is still so hot that the water round him boils up like a cauldron and a great cloud of steam goes up and hangs over the river.

But Zomo, he doesn't stop to watch. By the time old Kada disappears, he is already halfway to the palace to claim his reward.

The Great Tug-of-War

IT HAPPENS one year that the rains come late and go early so the harvest is poor and food is scarce. Animals who usually reap a hundred baskets of corn find they have only fifty, and animals who usually reap fifty find they have only twenty-five. As for Zomo, who never reaps more than ten, even in the best of seasons, he is left with only five.

"When are you going to fetch the rest of it?" asks his wife when he brings home his five baskets.

"There isn't any more," says Zomo.

"D'you mean to tell me," says his wife, "that this

114

is all we have to eat for the next twelve months?"

"We shall have to manage as best we can," says Zomo.

The corn lasts through most of the dry season but by the time the hot weather comes round, it is nearly finished. First Zomo tries to borrow some more, but the other animals say they have none to lend. Then he tries to borrow money so that he can buy corn in the market, but they remember the last time they lent him money, and so they are sorry but they can't oblige.

When his wife tells him that they have food for only two more days, Zomo reckons that the time has come for him to have a good think. So he goes and sits under the *chediya* tree with his thinking cap on, and in the evening, when his wife calls him in to supper, he tells her that he is going to go and see Giwa the Elephant, who has more corn than he knows what to do with.

Next morning, Zomo puts on his best gown and goes and calls on Giwa. When he reaches the house, he says that he has a message for the master and he is taken into the audience chamber where Giwa is receiving those who come to pay their respects.

"God give you long life," cries Zomo in a loud voice, doing obeisance and looking very respectful.

"Amen, Zomo," says Giwa, who likes to be buttered up.

"I have a message for you," says Zomo. "It is from Dorina the Hippopotamus."

"We don't see much of him since he's taken to

living in the river," says Giwa. "Tell me," he goes on, "does he still have that black stallion?"

"That is what the message is about," says Zomo.

"Well, you can tell him from me," says Giwa, "that if he still wants to swap the black for my chestnut, there is nothing doing; but I will buy the black from him any time he likes."

"He is short of corn this year," says Zomo, "and he says that if you can let him have some, he will give you the black in exchange."

"Oho," says Giwa, "so that's how the land lies, is it? Well, how much does he want?"

"He says that he'll let him go for a hundred baskets," says Zomo, "so long as he can keep him until after the festival."

"Whatever does he want to do that for?" asks Giwa.

"He's his favorite mount," says Zomo, "and he likes to ride him in the procession."

"All right," says Giwa, "tell Dorina it's a bargain."

Without more ado, the elephant orders his wife and daughters to measure out a hundred baskets of corn.

"There you are, Zomo," he says when this is done. "If you lead the way, my boys will carry it for you. And tell Dorina," he goes on, "that he can keep the black until the festival, but no longer."

"I'll tell him that," says Zomo. So saying, he takes his leave and sets off with ten young elephants behind him who are each carrying ten baskets of corn.

"All right, put it down here, boys," says Zomo when they reach a place near his house. "You've done your share—I'll get those lazy young hippos to take it the rest of the way."

As soon as the young elephants have gone, Zomo calls to his wife and children and they carry the baskets into his house. When they have finished, his corn-stores are all full and running over.

"Where did you get all this?" asks Zomo's wife when they finish carting the corn.

"Giwa is my friend," says Zomo, "and when he hears that my corn is nearly finished, he insists on giving me some of his. 'Zomo,' he says. 'I won't have you going short.' Naturally I do not wish to offend him and so I accept."

When she hears this, Zomo's wife looks at him as if she doesn't believe a word he says, but she holds her tongue and says nothing.

Next morning, Zomo puts on his best gown again, and this time he makes for the river where Dorina the Hippopotamus has his house. Since Dorina lives in the water, the bad season does not hurt him and he has plenty of food.

When Zomo reaches Dorina's gate, he says that he has a message for him and is taken to the audience chamber.

"God give you victory," Zomo cries in a loud voice, doing obeisance and looking very respectful, just as he does with the elephant.

"Welcome, Zomo," says Dorina. "What brings you to these parts?"

"I have a message," says Zomo, "from Giwa the Elephant."

"Oh?" says Dorina. "What does Giwa want with me?"

"He wants to know," says Zomo, "whether you still want to buy his chestnut."

"Of course I do," says Dorina. "I even offer to swap my black for him, but Giwa will not have it."

"Well, he's changed his mind now," says Zomo, and tells Dorina the same tale that he already told Giwa, right down to the bit about Giwa wishing to keep the chestnut until the festival because it is the horse he likes to ride in the procession. Dorina is so pleased with the proposition that then and there he tells his wife and daughters to prepare a hundred baskets of dried fish.

When the fish is ready, Zomo takes his leave and sets off for dry land with twenty young hippos behind him, each carrying five baskets. By and by they reach a place near his house, and he tells them to put the stuff down and he will get the young elephants, who are fat and lazy he says, to carry it the rest of the way.

As soon as the young hippos have gone back to the river, Zomo fetches his wife and children and they carry the baskets home. Since the larder is already full of corn, the eight youngest rabbits have to give up their hut to make room for the fish, which fills it right up to the thatch and makes it bulge like a pumpkin.

Soon after this, the rains come and all through the rainy season Zomo keeps his wife and children busy plaiting a rope. It is the biggest rope you ever saw and so strong that you can tie Giwa the Elephant up with it and he won't get loose. His old woman is always asking Zomo what they want with such a rope, but Zomo won't say.

By and by, when the rains are nearly over, the festival comes round. All the animals ride in the procession, and the elephant sees that the hippo is mounted on the black, and the hippo sees that the elephant is mounted on the chestnut.

Next day, bright and early, Zomo takes one end of his rope and sets out for the river. When he comes to the bank, he finds a fig tree and passes the rope round the trunk. Then he goes on to the hippo's house.

"Ah, Zomo," says Dorina when he is ushered into his presence, "you are just the man I wish to see. Do you bring news about my horse?"

"God give you long life," says Zomo, "here is the end of his tethering rope, which Giwa the Elephant tells me to bring to you. When the sun rises tomorrow, he will take him down to the river by the fig tree, and he says when you see the leaves of the fig tree begin to shake, it will be the signal to pull him in on the rope."

"Very well," says Dorina. "We'll be ready."

"God give you victory," Zomo goes on, "Giwa also says to tell you that this chestnut of his is a mighty strong horse and that he can't answer for it if you let him get away."

"Never fear," says Dorina, "my boys will take care of him."

When Zomo leaves the hippo, he goes and gets the other end of the rope and takes it to the elephant's house. "God give you long life," he says to Giwa, and then he spins him the same yarn, right down to the bit about the black being a mighty strong horse and Dorina not answering for it if he lets him get away.

"Not to worry," says Giwa. "My boys will look after him all right."

When Zomo gets home that evening, he tells his wife that people may come asking for him next day, and that if they do, she is to say that he is gone to Gwanja.

"But," says she, "you aren't going to Gwanja, are you?"

"Not I," says Zomo, "but this is what you must

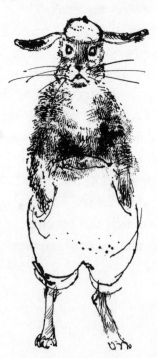

say. And furthermore," he goes on, "if they ask how long I shall be away, you are to say six months if not eight."

Early next morning, before the sun rises, Giwa the Elephant lines up his ten sons outside his house. He tells them that the hippo's black is mighty strong and that when he gives the signal they must heave on the rope with all their might. On the river bank Dorina the Hippo is doing the same thing with his twenty sons.

By and by the sun rises, the breeze springs up, and the leaves of all the trees along the river bank begin to shake. But Giwa and Dorina do not notice the other trees because they are only watching the fig tree. As soon as they see its leaves shaking, they both shout, "Heave," and then all the young elephants and all the young hippos begin to pull on the rope as if their lives depend on it.

At first the hippos gain some ground. When the old elephant sees this, he thinks that his horse is getting away and so he becomes very agitated and dances up and down and shouts to his sons to pull harder. Then the elephants begin to gain ground and it is the turn of the old hippo at the other end to become agitated and dance up and down and shout.

While this goes on, Zomo slips out of his house and hides himself in the branches of the fig tree. He has to hold on tight because the elephants and the hippos are pulling it this way and that and at one time he thinks that the tree will come up by the roots. But he waits until the tree is steady because both sides strain

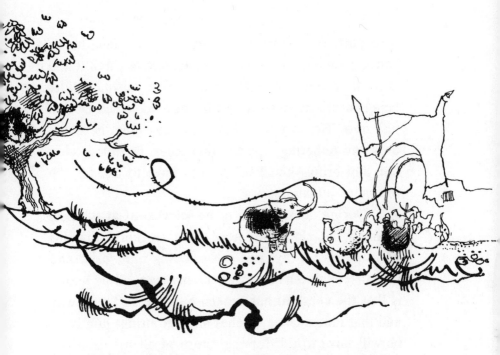

so hard, and then he takes out his knife and reaches down and cuts the rope.

When Zomo cuts the rope, the young hippos, who are up on the bank of the river, go toppling back into the water and make such a mighty splash that it stuns all the fish for miles around and even gives old Kada the Crocodile a headache.

As for the young elephants at the other end, they are right in front of their father's house, and so when the rope parts, they all go tumbling backward and knock down the ornamental gateway, which Giwa made for himself the year before, and then go rolling on into the compound where they flatten two huts and a corn-store.

When the old elephant and the old hippo see the

rope part, they both think they will lose their horse, and so they both dash out to the fig tree to catch it and there they run into one another. Now Giwa, besides being surprised, is by no means pleased to see Dorina just now. He scowls at him and says that the black broke his tethering rope and that unless Dorina catches him and brings him back he will have to ask for the return of all his corn.

Dorina doesn't care to be scowled at at the best of times, let alone just now when he thinks that his horse has got away, and so he scowls right back and says that he doesn't know about any corn, all he knows is that the chestnut has broken his rope and got away and that unless Giwa catches him and brings him back he will have to ask for the return of all his fish.

Giwa is not used to being spoken to like this, even by Zaki the Lion, and doesn't care for it any more than Dorina cares to be scowled at. "Dorina," he says, "you get above yourself. You may be a great man among the frogs and fishes, but here on land we don't consider you any great shakes."

This makes Dorina madder than ever because he doesn't like to be reminded that he now lives with frogs and fishes. "Giwa," he says, "the only reason I leave dry land and live in the water is that your belly rumbles so loud at night that it disturbs my children and they don't get their proper sleep."

At this, Giwa calls the hippo a baseborn, bandy-legged bog-trotter, and Dorina says that the elephant is a beady-eyed, swivel-nosed, loppy-lugged lounge-about. If the other animals don't come running up at this moment, they will certainly come to blows but as it is, they are just parted in time.

Later both of them send for Zomo, but they are told that Zomo is gone to Gwanja and won't be back for six months, if not eight. In fact it is much longer than this before Giwa and Dorina are on speaking terms again.

As for Zomo, he lies low and keeps out of everybody's sight. But his wife and children get so fat on Giwa's corn and Dorina's fish that the other animals think that Zomo must be working in Gwanja and sending money back to his family.

"That Zomo," they say to one another, "I do declare that he has turned over a new leaf at last."

Publisher's Note on
Zomo's Origins

ZOMO is a disreputable but authentic character of African folklore. He originally came from Hausaland, in what is now Northern Nigeria, but cousins of his, equally unscrupulous and no less engaging, are to be found in many other parts of the continent. These rascally rabbits (or to be more precise, hares) take the leading parts in many African narratives.

Although these stories and scores of others like them have been told around the firesides of Africa for hundreds and hundreds of years, literal translations of them do not read well. For one thing, Zomo has to share the star parts with other characters like the jackal

127

and the spider and so there are too many different heroes. Another problem is that the texts of literal translations are usually stark and bald. The reason for this is that the African narrators act all the parts and throw in stage and sound effects for good measure. Because the printed word lacks these aids, it suffers from the want of embroidery. Finally there is the awkward fact that many of the original endings are so bloody that, in an anthology like this one, the author would either run out of characters or else be forced into the contradiction of resurrecting them after each demise.

To overcome these difficulties, the author has felt justified in discarding the less attractive heroes and awarding their parts to Zomo, modifying some of the plots, and supplying some of the missing verbal embroidery. In taking these liberties, however, he has done his best to preserve the authentic African atmosphere of the strange court over which that rather dull-witted monarch, Zaki the Lion, traditionally presides. And he has told the tales as much as possible in the present tense, suggesting the flavor of the original story-teller's language which has little or no past tense.

In making his adaptations, the author has ample precedent, for when the Hausa people came to America as slaves, they brought with them their stories. As these stories were told and retold in this country, Brer Rabbit became the hero of most of them, and gradually the stories themselves changed, too. But over the years and through many tellings, the character himself, with his genius for skulduggery and mayhem, did not.